Other books by Richard Elman

FICTION
Little Lives *(as John Howland Spyker)*
Taxi Driver *(with Paul Schrader)*
Fredi & Shirl & the Kids: The Autobiography in Fables of Richard M. Elman: A Novel
Crossing Over
An Education in Blood
The Reckoning
Lilo's Diary
The 28th Day of Elul
A Coat For the Tsar

NONFICTION
Uptight with the Rolling Stones
Charles Booth's London *(with Albert Fried)*
Ill-at-Ease in Compton
The Poorhouse State: The American Way of Life on Public Assistance

POETRY
Homage to Fats Novarro
The Man Who Ate New York

The Breadfruit Lotteries

The Breadfruit Lotteries

A Novel | Richard Elman

Richard Elman
3 March, 1980

Methuen New York · London · Toronto · Sydney

Copyright © 1980 by Richard Elman
All rights reserved,
No part of this publication may be reproduced, stored
in a retrieval system or transmitted in any form or
by any means, electronic, mechanical, photocopying,
recording, or otherwise, without the prior permission
of the publisher.

Manufactured in the United States of America
First Edition
Published in the United States of America by
Methuen, Inc.
733 Third Avenue
New York, N.Y. 10017
Designed by Jacqueline Schuman

Library of Congress Cataloging in Publication Data
Elman, Richard M
  The breadfruit lotteries.
  I. Title.
PZ4.E475Br 1980 [PS3555.L628] 813'.5'4 79-20725
ISBN 0-416-00541-1

for my colleagues
&
A

"Ripe buku (breadfruit) no good fe pickny,"
Jamaica Talk by Frederic G. Cassidy

"*Faux naivete*: a way of thinking displeasing to the Agency."
Henderson Blaine in
A Dictionary of Company Acronyms

Author's Note: This is said to be a work of fiction. Any resemblance to real persons living or dead is strictly coincidental, with the exception of names that have been reported in news stories through the media.

According to the Select Committee to Investigate Intelligence, in its report issued by Senator Frank Church, a very large number of American academics *have* served as undercover operatives of the Central Intelligence Agency.

It is only a matter of imagination for an author to consider what might happen to one such academic, under the circumstances.

Richard Elman
Isola Di Ponza
Italy
11 April, 1979

The Breadfruit Lotteries

WE WERE DRIVING at medium speed along the southern coast of the island. Not too far east of Morant Bay, Dyllis shook out her beautiful long auburn hair, as if a sudden chill had gotten to her. She asked if we could find a place to spend the night.

"It's probably just jet lag Rob," she told me, "I'm beat. Can't we call it a day?"

It was only 3:00 P.M., and I was feeling pretty turned around myself. They steer on the wrong side of the road in Jamaica; British-style motoring takes getting used to, if you've just arrived by plane, as we had, and gone off to the car rental immediately for the run across island all the way to Port Antonio before nightfall.

Perhaps we should have stayed on in Kingston for another day and rested, but I wasn't feeling up to being in that huge disorderly city so early in our vacation together.

The storm of worries I'd left behind in New York that spring, which I was trying hard to keep out of mind, were vocational but also personal: a close friend and colleague had flipped out after accusing half the intellectual establishment, including most of our mutual friends and colleagues on the Upper West Side, of working for the CIA. As a History of Ideas man with some practical Poli-Sci background, I'd been selected to evaluate his charges for an intra-faculty disciplinary committee. There were certain dossiers in my suitcase that I'd have to review in a value-free way later on in the holiday, though frankly, I found Blake's data unconvincing, and insufficient. As much as I sympathized with my friend's general point of view—and had even thought of writing a longish essay-review or a monograph on the subject myself—I was discreetly aware such billingsgate had, at best, only subjective reality.

So I was just very glad to get away from so much acrimony for awhile with this beautiful young woman friend; and as I concentrated on driving around those curvy roads in all that heat and dust the harsh voices of my colleagues with their allegations at our eternal committee meetings were banished by balmy salt breezes, the swaying of palm and eucalyptus.

Nothing like tropical balm to ventilate a good Protestant conscience, though Dyllis still seemed a little impatient with me. "Watch for traffic Rob," she said, when I drapped an arm across her shoulders as we passed through a grove of stunted banana cultivations; some swollen bright red prepuces climbing toward broad green underleaves seemed about to burst with flowers.

And whenever I got near to 40 mph Dyllis reminded me as to how there was a governor on the accelerator, and about the Jamaica price of an Imperial gallon of petrol.

"I'm really fagged," she said. "Snookered, Rob, I should say. Can't we take a breather and go on in the morning?"

We moved through cane breaks, gross thickets of Indian shot, and turkey weed. No real rest spots anywhere.

"Tell you what," I said to her, "When we get back to the City I'll have old Blake over for drinks, or coffee, and a chat. Maybe I can convince him to withdraw his manuscript from the Review in its present form by offering to collaborate with him at a later date. . . ."

"Fat chance," Dyllis said. "Not hardly likely, I should say."

The man's just mad, Rob, and a cad to boot. Ask any of his female students what he's been up to. For us to be spending our hard-earned holiday in the sun thinking of his delusionary behavior is an imposition, I should say. . . ."

"It happens to be my job," I reminded Dyllis.

"So am I at present, Rob," she smirked. "Don't you remember?"

Dyllis had been my second-best graduate student. We'd only gotten on a more intimate basis in the last fortnight or so. But now that we were together for fun she sometimes functioned more like the teacher, a pretty stern taskmaster: when she wanted something, she really had to have it.

She said, "When I'm off like this I can get to be a real layabout. . . ."

"I should hope so," I murmured back.

"I could get really feverish, Rob," she told me.

Such an enticing foxy number: that buttery smile, and that lovely long leggy body.

You had to be entirely wiped out, and she too, before you even dared to enter any hotel room alone with such a bird as she. It just wouldn't ever do to be so-so beat; there'd be squabbles, about needs and wants.

Dyllis was Anglo-Arab, from a Bajan diplomatic family. Going to Jamaica on holiday with her was the next best thing, I supposed, to a proper visit with her family in Barbados. That just wasn't possible. I was a quarter of a century older: Our excuse for going away together had to be her dissertation; it was all I could do to remind her we had planned a restful time together, and she still had some reading to do for her orals.

"It won't be dark for a couple of hours yet," I added, "and we've got guaranteed reservations in Port Antonio."

"Even so . . . " She yawned, as if she'd been kissed by all

that heavy moist heat. "I've had too much sun Rob, I . . ."

"I know you're tired. . . ." To fill in the word for her this time, as if it were one of the slots in some graduate exam I'd tutored her for, gave me a sort of consoling relief. It was also true I was enjoying the green wash of Jamaican landscape across my eyes.

"Love," I told her, "try to imagine yourself in the old colonial times as one of those great ladies or white witches with Mandingo slaves."

"With my complexion?" She laughed, a little harshly, "Not hardly likely."

Dyllis was glowing, rosy, a dusky rose.

We swerved about a bare mossy-green promontory over the sea.

"How lovely, Rob," she said. "Compared to this, Barbados always seems so flat. I just know it's going to be really nice for us here. Fun, and I'll be patient. You'll see. I'm trying. . . ."

Which meant she was giving me maybe fifteen or twenty minutes grace, not more, and not quite enough since there just didn't seem to be any inns, hotels, or motels on this part of the island; just mile after mile of small dusty farmhouses under coconut palms, kitchen gardens full of climbing yams, groves of banana and papaya, black ackees rotting thickly by the roadside under gum tree shade; and the sea, so very deep, dusted a blue-grey-green, as if wiped over with pastels. Where it cut deeply into all the promontories of the land every few miles or so, it gave off a rank sweet odor.

Such abundant local traffic inhibited speed. Toward twilight Dyllis asked, "What do you suppose we'll do tomorrow?"

"Swim, Eat, Sleep," I said. "Drink. Make love. What else? You can read if you like. I just may try fishing."

A couple of ugly black John Crow vultures with swollen

purplish beaks flapped dark shadows off their large wings against the Mini Cooper's front windshields.

We both flinched a little as I sped on.

Dyllis said, "Who is it you wanted to see anyway over to Port Antonio?"

"McAvoy recommended the place to me a long time ago. He said it was a lot less touristy than Ocho Rios or Montego."

"*Terrif*." As she glanced out the window at a squalid collection of shacks we were passing, I flinched again from her sarcasm, a tin roof in a sudden windstorm.

Dyllis said, "Mac wanting you to go native is a little *foo-foo*, if you ask me."

I didn't like Dyllis bad-mouthing Mac. He had a really first-class mind. Perhaps Mac played around a bit too much, but I liked him hugely. My number one ace graduate student until he left to do other things at home connected to the family business, Mac *was* a charmer; and I hoped we would see each other sometime during the trip, though for now he was in Manderville, with his wealthy family, at their ranch.

He'd told me once there were many McAvoys in Jamaica, but only one family, his own, had married with the Carter-Groves and sent their kids off to prep school at Hotchkiss. "Compared to us," he used to say, "people like the Manleys are just a bunch of climbing octaroons, and macaroons, and nectarines. We've got Bourbon in our blood, mon, meaning the French, not the whiskey."

Mac also enjoyed a good gossip. Most West Indians do, I think.

Dyllis, who could be terribly snobby at times, sometimes called him "Granny."

Now she said, "Would it please you to know if Granny and I had ever been lovers?"

"Indeed it would *not*, deary." Why was she being such a brat? Thinking about the cool breezes of the mountains around Manderville, I yawned, and added, "You upper class types in the Caribbean are all descended from the same spider."

"Hah." It was more like a dare than a laugh, and the heat inside the sedan was making me so groggy I pressed down hard on the accelerator, an automaton.

The car leaped forward and swerved, almost off the road. "Easy Robert," Dyllis went. I should have asked her to drive.

An hour or so later it was dark, and cooler, and that's when I spotted the old motel, dumped down on the beach, with the trade winds beginning to blow, beneath a large flowering almond tree. We were in a place called Long Bay. Not much there except a few scabby houses, a post office, and this one motel.

I jammed down hard on the brakes.

"Looks cozy, no?"

"So nice . . ." she said, "It's just like in a movie. Do you think they'll have a room? It seems pretty much abandoned."

"Just the way I feel Dyllis . . . No harm looking around . . ."

Twenty paces from the surf, a series of one-story concrete bungalows clustered around a patio and open bar, under tile roofs, and moorish bits of trim. Seen from the fragrant outer darkness, the bar itself was without any bottled stock, just a lot of broken glassware on the shelves; it was circular and faced all around with large tortoise shells, like suits of armor, and there were even more of these carapaces in the corners of the large, damp patio, lit by only a single dim yellow bulb, above the shiny steel bar sink.

Almond, honeysuckle, and frangipani mixed their odors as we walked out into the warm night air, arm in arm. I could see the dark outlines of two men sprawling across the curbstones at the entranceway.

"Good evening," I greeted them.

"Closed," said the older of the two, "we be *out* of business now." Had a very dark face, and wore shorts, through which a yellow plastic artificial limb poked at me like a weapon. Even leaning asprawl he had a certain military bearing, an aplomb, such as one might expect from a British colonial noncom.

I came a little closer with Dyllis, now hand in hand.

"*Fe* what you want here, sir?" asked the other fellow, who was smaller, dark suited with an open collar, and quite lean, tan-colored.

The low sloshy pounding of surf convinced me this was just the place to spend the night.

"We're Americans, my wife and I," I lied, "and while driving by we saw the place and it looked kind of inviting. We just want to rest and swim in the morning." I added: "Do you know how we could speak to the owners?"

"I be the manager," said the first. "Tell you what, it cannot be done. We have no insurance . . . and no more license. . . .

"Look about you," he gestured, "it is all rather coming apart and desolated."

It did look a little like the better parts of Folly Beach, South Carolina. I started to pull Dyllis away.

Then the second one said something in Creole. Sounded like *duppy*. Or *dippy*.

"Wait Bob," she said, touching my arm.

The thin man spoke: "If you stay here you won't like it a bit sir, madame, as the place has gotten to be just a little musty and out of hand with centipedes everywhere and you will end up making monkey faces to each other."

"We're not scared," Dyllis said. "We don't want luxuries."

"There's nothing to eat here, or drink," said the thin, tan man again, "until breakfast tomorrow morning down at the inn. That's about two kilometers from here . . . due west. . . . You may have passed it?"

"I don't recall."

Dyllis said, "We really would like to stay here."

The dark man grinned, and giggled a little: "*Ooooo* . . ." Then he brought himself to attention: "Well, sir, *fe* the room you will have to register at the bar, with your driving papers, and then, if you have a torch, I will be happy to show you to your bungalow. It's right down on the *plage*. Can't miss it. . . ."

He made so much of that French word I felt certain he'd been overseas.

Said, "Thank you." Asked by way of making conversation if he'd lost the limb at Kaiserine Pass.

"Why do you wish to know, sir?"

"Because I was there, too, and the Colonial troops always fought best."

"Always the case, US," he grinned again. Showed me a musty old register book at the bar in which I scribbled out my name and address, along with Mr. & Mrs. We were the first to register, I noticed, in over two years.

"What happened around here?" I asked, pointing to the lines of sharply broken glassware on the shelf above the bar. It reminded me of the tops of brick walls at my old boarding school: Colby. You climbed over late at night and got your hands all cut up.

From somewhere behind me in the dark the tan man was answering: "American people. They got frightened and left before they could sell. Now George here and I manage for them. You know we just look after their property . . . tings. . . ."

He came close, and looked at me, very soberly, and then he giggled, and so did George.

"Dey left ASAP," he added. "Dat's Midwest for as soon as possible," and giggled again at my face.

I asked how much we would have to pay for the room.

"Twenty dollar Jamaican," George said, which seemed rather like a lot, and my face must have registered a certain dismay in the dim light, because he added: "It is not beyond your means, is it, sir, because there is a lovely beach, no sharks, not even a mongoose hereabouts, and you can swim all day, even naked a little further down, if you like, and if you stay more than one night de rates go down."

"*Nobody* here to bother you," the tan man added, as if I was still making up my mind. "De four extra dollars are *fe* sheets."

I found a traveler's check and signed my name and gave it to George who said, "Gladly, sir . . ."

Dyllis had already started to walk back down toward the car to find a flashlight.

Guided by the yellow eye of light, she searched the car for our handbags, preparatory to coming toward us again.

"Pretty woman you have, "George said. "She be . . ."

". . . Bajan."

"You have nothing to worry about here mon," said the tan man, from my other side. "Long Bay it be a very peaceful place right now. No more trouble here . . . just bananas. . . ."

Again he was laughing.

George corrected him: "Tell him we have the *Gros Michel* Banana."

Tan man seemed to think that was very witty, too.

He said to me, "Sir, we have so many good things here. Are you a fisherman? We have the kingfish, the blackfish, the Jewfish . . . and we have the *lignum vitae*, or we call it bullet wood, which is *the* hardest wood in whole wide world." As he laughed again, George made a gesture toward a certain part of his body that was also known to harden. I hoped only I could see what he was doing.

"That's alright fellows," Dyllis said, "it's only me."

Clearing his throat loudly, George showed us along the path of light to our bungalow.

"Dis one cottage spic and span is always kept for de honeymooners," he said, as if grinning again.

"Goodnight sir, dame."

Up a few steps was a porch, and a small glass louvered door which opened with a key.

The room we entered was bare and dingy; it smelled of almond blossom and Saniflush.

Dyllis threw herself right down on the bed.

"You know, Rob," she said, "we ought to make the most of tonight as this may be the only proper honeymoon cottage I'll ever get to stay in."

I had not yet turned off the flash and its light across her face softened her cheeks and left her smile dissolute.

As soon as I shut the door I fell down next to her, and we clung together in a hot squirming of the flesh, so that when sleep came at last it was like being smothered by a heavy dark hand that was also trying to help me remove a hair shirt.

FASTIDIOUSLY BLACK, if you please, in crisp pressed whites, Deputy Inspector Larsen stood outside the door addressing us early the next morning, his eyes large, wide, tinted violet: "Am I calling on the temporary bungalow residence of Professor Robert Harmon?"

After giving three sharp raps to our front door, he added softly, as if it were an afterthought, "Police sir, open up."

Dyllis immediately rushed naked for the bathroom.

I already had on my walking shorts so I went barechested toward the door.

"What seems to be the trouble?" Inquired with the door still closed.

"No problem, sir, if you're Harmon."

The latch released, I caught a glimpse of a shiny new black-and-white police vehicle parked inside the patio, alongside the bar; a second copper in the driver's seat was mopping at his brow while a red-and-yellow siren light revolved silently overhead.

Larsen was not a small man, but because he dressed so impeccably he appeared trim, without any flab. In all the heat of that bright, drenching sun his brow seemed dry, unfurrowed, but his smile had a certain formalistic flash, right on, and then off again, like the standard English he spoke at me; I knew he did not speak that way with his fellow countrymen. He wore black lizard sandals over white sweat socks.

"Sir, would your name be Professor Robert Har*mon*?"

There happened to be nobody else standing in my doorway.

"My wife's dressing," I explained. "What can I do for you?"

"If you don't mind stepping out on the steps of your bungalow, sir." He carried a sidearm in a shiny black holster. I didn't recognize the make or caliber.

"What seems to be the trouble, officer?"

"I should like to examine those papers you showed the man here last night."

"Is anything wrong?"

When I gave George my traveler's check I had simply displayed my driver's license for ID.

Another sort of quick-erase grimace from Larsen: "Jamaica is a very small island, sir. It is also a sovereign nation state. If you have nothing to worry about you should be prompt to oblige me as an authority figure and step outside."

"Just a sec. I'll fetch what I've got."

I went in to get our passports, which we were keeping separate, and when I returned I saw George, the peg-legged fellow, who had shown us to our rooms last night, crossing the patio with a bottle of frosted coke for the other damp cop. George walked as if on parade, strutting, bad leg, and all.

I was wearing my blue net shirt when I handed our papers over to Larsen.

Carefully, he glanced through each passport.

"You're not married?"

"It seemed more convenient to refer to our arrangement in that manner," I said. "You understand. We didn't quite know what to expect down here."

"So you lied?" Larsen concluded my remarks with an accusation. I nodded back.

He waited, as if to let my guilt sink in.

Then he said, "In the States you teach university, Mr. Single Professor?"

"*Yes.*"

"Which one?"

"Columbia."

"In the City of New York?"

"That's correct, sir." I hoped he was enjoying my deference: "Seriously, what's the trouble? What seems to be wrong?"

"Do you ever use ganja or cocaine?"

"No sir."

I felt very like a schoolkid.

"Sure?"

"Quite!"

"No lying again?"

I nodded.

He didn't seem to want to check me out any further about that one.

Larsen glanced again at our passports as Dyllis, dressed and groomed in jodphurs and a teal blue silk blouse, like somebody in a fashion photo for *Town & Country*, came to join us.

"Your wife?" He was smirking.

"We've been together," I said, "for a little while. . . ."

"What's all this about?" Dyllis asked, with British contempt.

"Sister, you be quiet," Larsen said. "I'm afraid I shall have to ask you to come with me immediately to Port Antonio, Professor."

I felt scared.

"What's happening?" she demanded. "What has he done?"

No use in arguing with a man who wore a gun.

"You will explain, of course," I said, "as we go?"

"Afraid I can't sir, right at the moment," Larsen said. "In any event, I shall have to ask you to come, Professor."

"*Why?*" Dyllis was piercing. "*What have we done?*"

"*Not you sister*," he said. "It's your boyfriend the Professor we care about. There's some sort of inquiry from Kingston out about him on the telex."

"But we're here for vacation," I pointed out.

"Very sad to hear that so; you'll have to come anyway. With any luck you should be back by teatime, or nightfall. Meantime," Larsen grinned at me again, like a chalk mark suddenly scratched on a blackboard, so that I shivered a little, "going to have to ask my man *fe* to go through your Mini for weapons."

3

THERE USED TO be an expression: "It's your funeral."

I felt that way during the drive with Larsen.

"It's your funeral," I told myself, over and again. Don't know what I meant.

It was as if I'd been indiscreet somehow when I wasn't.

But I must have been. Done something wrong.

Damned if I knew what.

Under the terms of the Jamaican Gun Court law, enacted a few years back to deter armed gangsterism, all persons found with unlicensed weapons on the island could be kept indefinitely in a detention center.

I had in my car a Swiss army knife and a tire jack.

Could they be considered at all lethal?

I pictured myself languishing for many years behind pallisades and guard towers in the Jamaican sun and dust.

Or suppose they had planted something on me? Ganja? or other contraband?

Our drive took the better part of an hour. Mostly lush, and pleasant scenery all the way, only I couldn't really bring myself to look out the windows like any ordinary tourist.

Nobody spoke to me.

No further explanations.

The only other time I had felt so frightened was in France

once, during the War, when I'd had to parachute out of a Liberator: "C'est votre funérailles Harmon," I'd told myself then, unable even to use the possessive *mon*.

During the drive, Inspector Larsen and his deputy sat up front; I was put in the back, in a caged-off area. A riot shotgun was mounted in between us, on the ceiling, along with tear gas cannisters. Occasionally the radio burst in on our silence, garbled sounds, or fusillades of static.

We went through patched and shabby villages, passed an occasional elegant villa, perched high and white and cool on a bluff.

All ages, colors, and conditions of people were gawking at us from the roadways, or in the cramped little buses we overtook. They must be wondering who I am, I thought: some big shot, perhaps, head of the whole inter-island traffic.

Once we came to Port Antonio the deputy turned on his siren and we wailed our way through narrow, dusty streets straight toward the principal square and the police station. Parked.

I was let out of my cage, and, with both gentlemen at my side, guided into headquarters, and around past a small docket, where there was much palaver going, to another large bare room with a square table, and chairs pulled up beneath. The blinds on all the windows were open, letting in heat as well as light. An old black ceiling fan turned slowly, the daylight seeming to flicker on and off with its revolutions.

Somebody called out: "Looks like you've got yourself a Bogey."

"Easy does it," Larsen told him, unbuckling himself of his weapon.

He asked me to sit down, if I liked. My shorts and shirt were drenching. I'd been sweating more than I'd realized.

He said, "Professor, you wait and watch the fan go round

and round and take it slow. Everything here is copacetic. Chief will want to talk to you himself."

He bowed before a water cooler, sipped, and then left the room.

Moments later a good looking, coffee-colored man in a snappy sand-colored military tunic, and knee shorts, stepped into the room, his great wide face open and earnest, mocha thighs abulge. To tell me to stay seated he held up one hand. *So...*

His fingers were long, delicate, chin and nose finely cut, Dravidian. When I was able to look more closely at the Brigadier, I noticed his sideburns were rather long, with a reddish sheen.

He identified himself as being of that rank, said the name was "Erskine..."

"Pleased," I started to rise again, "I'm sure. But why am I here?"

"You are not Professor Robert Harmon of Columbia University?"

"I most certainly am, sir."

"Don't sir me, Professor. You teach politics?"

"History and politics..." As if confessing: "I'm afraid I'm rather academic."

"And you served with the Office of Strategic Services during World War II?"

"That certainly was no crime, *then* ... thirty years ago...."

"Perhaps not." The Brigadier paced hither and yon, his hands joined at the small of his back.

"Do you know a Mister St. John McAvoy?"

Turning fan blades gave off a sudden loud black whirring, and then clacked, and whirred again, as if increasing speed. *Mac in trouble? How?*

With my head still bowed, as if confronting an executioner's sword, I would say nothing to Erskine about my student.

"You do in fact know McAvoy," said the Brigadier. "Answer me please, Professor."

"I know Mac, yes. He's a very funny guy."

"You think so? How?" With his fist, Erskine suppressed a grin.

Until I knew more I would say no more.

It could be Mac was being a prankster through some of his upperclass connections.

Erskine said, "The Detainee avers he was well acquainted with the late St. John McAvoy."

"Is Mac in any trouble?" I inquired.

"I shall ask all the questions, Professor." The Brigadier seemed quite annoyed with me: "Did you have plans to see your good friend, Mac, as you've called him, this very trip?"

A queasy stomach sort of candor must have shown on my face.

"You will please answer, please. Did you plan to see McAvoy?"

"Yes I did."

Erskine seemed to exhale and grin all at once so that his military bearing, for a moment, came apart on him, and he seemed to be slouching over a very small pot belly.

"That probably won't be possible, Professor," Erskine told me, pulling himself up short and flat again: "You see Mr. McAvoy was critically wounded last night trying to assassinate our Prime Minister, Mr. Manley."

4

I SURPRISED MYSELF with my own tears. Mac had been so good to me. To everybody in New York. He couldn't assassinate anybody. He was just a bright playboy, I guess, not a very serious person. Just another nice bloke, though brainy enough, *Ok*, if you know what I mean.

But Brigadier Erskine glanced at me as if he was absolutely certain he was not telling me any news I didn't already know.

Recalling the flash of Mac's dark, handsome face made me shudder. Mac had taught me how to boogie at parties. That's how I came to meet Dyllis. Was she also his girl then? I really didn't think I cared to know.

I asked, "Are you saying he's been shot dead Brigadier?"

"Perforce I'm afraid so, Professor. Better him than our Mr. Manley."

He paced to the other side of that room again.

I just felt very sad, and tired.

The Brigadier asked, "*Now* would you care to make a statement?"

"I never knew Mac was political," I said, immediately hating myself for squirming so.

"So you don't tink he was political?" The Brigadier's look was quizzical, as if what I said had merely been the occasion for him to bat it back at my face.

He actually didn't seem to believe me. Said, "Isn't that rather odd, Professor, considering that you teach poli . . .?"

"*Political history,*" I corrected him, again. "*Political Science . . .Ideas . . .*"

"*. . . Which is not like politics?*" He seemed genuinely amused.

"I wish I could be of more help," I said, "but I really can't. I haven't been in touch with Mac for three months. I was going to suprise him, you see. This was purely a vacation for Dyllis, the lady, and me."

Erskine grunted.

He sat down at the other end of the table and began drumming on it with well-manicured fingernails.

"What kind of service did you see in the OSS?"

"That was more than thirty years ago."

"Nevertheless," he said, "you will answer the question."

My friend was dead. The loss was pain, like being hurt myself.

I had nothing to tell Erskine that could help. These were my country's thirty-year-old and best-kept secrets, but they were also *my* secrets: of ways I'd hoped I would never have to be again.

I tried to make it all sound offhand: "Wasn't quite routine stuff, if you know what I mean. We were covert ops, clandestines, rather on the dark side."

I found my fists clenched tightly and went on: "It was a long time ago. I was just another bright kid from Yale. Europe, the Middle East . . ."

"But what did you do?" Erskine demanded.

"Effectively we killed, but only combatants," I added. "I never was an assassin."

"A fine distinction I suppose." He seemed to be sneering at me.

"Anyway," I told him, "we did mostly black stuff. Propaganda. Black. Stuff of that sort to that effect . . .

"Brigadier," I added, frustrated with my own failure to seem more open, or specific, "I had no connection to the so-called Crown Jewels. My hobbies are writing, cooking, and gardening, not spying. I am an intellectual."

Erskine heard me out, like judge and jury. As his fingers tattooed the wood again he became my prosecutor: "According to Professor Billings Blake of your own Columbia University, in an unpublished paper, 'The following writers and intellectuals were all once part-time spies,' he intoned: 'In days of yore, Lord Byron, Daniel *De*foe, *Ru*dyard Kipling, Somerset Maugham, John Buchan . . . Graham Greene. . . .' "

"Are you saying I'm in good company?"

My joke fell flat.

With his eyes half shut Erskine continued this recital: " 'Dante Alighieri, John Milton, Andrew Marvell . . . H.A.R. (Kim) Philby . . . .' "

"Wrong side," I pointed out. "He was KGB. . . ."

"He doubled," Erskine said, as if correcting me. "More recently there was also the late T.S. Eliot, your own Mr. Peter Matthiesen, and the various editors of *Encounter* magazine in Great Britain."

"That may be so," I said, "but I am not. I am a guest here and my sympathies are with the aspirations of the Jamaican people. I swear. I consider myself a rather mild socialist. Blake's barmy, if you ask me."

"I *am* asking you, Professor. Is that why you have annotated so much of his paper? We found a holograph copy in one of your cases."

Erskine said, "If you really thought it was all blarney why study what he wrote so closely?"

Although I was fairly desperate to stop him from building a case against me, I didn't think I could explain confidential Columbia faculty business to a mere cop without getting myself in for even more trouble.

"*Who would ask me to spy?*" I demanded finally. "*Why?*"

"Very well," Erskine said, making that abrupt gesture with his hand when he'd heard enough.

"You have no call to get hysterical with me because of the company you keep, Professor." Erskine's smile was triumphant: "We do our homework down here in Jamaica. Did I mention Malcolm Muggeridge?"

"What about him?"

"He was also a spy like you," he said. "As you can see I have made quite a large study of intellectual and literary spies, independent of Professor Blake. Did my honors paper appropo that at Mona . . . took the tripos in intellectual history, as it's called . . . ."

"Very interesting," I said. "I apologize for thinking of you as a policeman."

"O I am that, too," he said. "Just another dumb copper, as you say, come a cropper. Don't you find that rather spooky?"

He grinned and looked away when he pressed a small white button on the arm of his chair. A young policeman appeared immediately in the doorway.

"This is Professor Robert Harmon, clandestine operative of the United States Central Intelligence Agency. Put him in one of the holding pens."

The boy snapped to. I shouted, *"Wait a mo—"*

Erskine spoke softly, "Later, Harmon, there'll be plenty of time for rebuttal, sur-rebuttal. Dismissed."

"What exactly are you charging me with? What do you say I've done?"

"Professor asks what?" Erskine laughed hoarsely. "You

work for the Company, sir. You conspired with McAvoy to assassinate our Mr. Manley on behalf of your CIA. Enough sir?"

"You're crazy, mon!"

A hand was gripping my bicep tightly, so that it ached. I was pulled toward the door at my back.

"I want a lawyer," I told him, "and you will have to notify my wife."

"Must we continue that masquerade?"

Erskine stood up: "Just go along and do as you're told, Professor, and I promise you you won't end up before a firing squad."

"I DEMAND TO SEE A REPRESENTATIVE OF THE UNITED STATES GOV. . . ."

A stunning heavy blow to the side of my face released me from the grip of that hand so that I began to blur all over even as I was falling face down toward the muddle of my extenuating circumstances.

5

THE CROCUS SACKS on which I'd just been laid out, like a stiff, must once have contained allspice, cinnamon, perhaps coffee, a good smell intermixing with that of the open five-gallon barrel for shit in the corner.

Underground, it was so very damp, and dark, except for the overhead grating on which black people padded, pink-footed. The only light came from a corner of overhead grid cubed by the brilliant sun.

My right jaw ached. Thoughts of calling out to the passersby were easily suppressed by my obvious disarray.

When I stood up I also felt dizzy. I was quite hungry; it had been a day, at least, since I'd eaten anything solid. Groggy, I thought I'd been drugged.

I searched the pockets of my shorts, but they were empty, too. Soggy all over, I waited, and sweated.

Presently I became aware of the presence of another person in that cell.

From the large galvanized barrel a pair of big shoes grew upside down. Next to it, this figure hunched and lurched forward, suddenly, toward me, on his knees.

"Woe is me," said a cracked phlegmy voice: *"Vey is mir.* I feel like a prisoner in a Bernard Malamud novel."

Light from the grating seemed to streak across his face. He was bearded, matted-looking, unkempt. A darkish long brown caftan hung from his hulking body like a Franciscan's habit, or the coarsely-woven garments of the Rastas. His fair face was cragged, with recondite features, as in certain Old Testament illustrations.

When I came a little closer and crouched in front of him, a heavy sweet rotten odor clogged my nostrils. There was a little tin basin of water by his side, and I wet the hem of my shirt and bathed his forehead.

He sighed piteously, profoundly.

"You're feeling better?" I asked.

"What do you think? I got caught, just like you. To tell you the truth it's been so long I can't remember all the details."

He reached out and took my face between his clammy hands and whispered into my ears, "Potok's my name, religion was my game. . . . Tell me something, soul brother," he demanded. "Did you get in all this trouble down here for sex, or money?"

"Neither quite," I pulled away from his hands and his stench.

"If you didn't do it for sex or money," Potok said, "it probably wasn't worth doing."

"Possibly . . ."

I had not previously experienced so much frankness from a man of God. Potok glanced over toward the barrel and asked: "Do you have to go?"

I said I most certainly did not.

"You sure?"

"Sure I'm sure."

"Good boy."

"Go to hell!"

"*Aumein,*" went Potok. "Attaboy. Keep it all to yourself, as there's somebody occupying the barrel presently."

"Besides," he added, "blood is thicker than water, as bread is thicker than butter . . . or even peanut butter *alavei*. . . ."

I turned away from him, and went back to the other side of my cell, to be with myself awhile.

I now think even if I had believed that it was the corpse of my friend McAvoy in that barrel, I would not have cared to look at him so displayed. I didn't think I had a single thing more to say to any person, living or dead. My friend was now a corpse, garbage, upside down in the shit. So undignified is death for some, I thought, it is not false pride that makes us wish to live forever.

This strange high-pitched keening interrupted my ruminations. It was mournful, and exhausting. On and on, Potok ullulated, and caterwauled, making crazy gurgling noises, and sounds, and finally breaking into a prayer-like intoning of song:

> "*I been a wandering
> early and late
> New York City
> and de Golden Gate
> and it looks like
> I'm never gonna
> stop
> my wandering . . .*"

"It looks to me like they just stopped you," I told him then: "Right down here in Jamaica. . . ."

"Look who's talking," he said: "The humane professor who screws his graduate students. *Bulvan!* . . .

> *"My sister was an engineer*
> *My father drove a hack*
> *My mother took in laundry*

"What's the matter?" he suddenly interrupted himself to inquire: "DON'T YOU LIKE?"

"I just don't get it," I said, "and I refuse to relate to any of this. I've got problems enough of my own. . . ."

From his foul dark corner Potok shrugged, as if he loathed himself for offering me only admonitions.

"You're probably guilty of something or other anyway," he said, "which I've tried to enumerate. So why not confess? We'll put it on your immortal expense account and it will save us all a lot of time."

Which made me feel all the more covetous for food to stuff my mouth, a great big bloody rare roast beef sandwich and a Red Cap.

"Potok," I said with a certain real hostility, "you stink!"

"It's not me, it's that barrel over there." Again he was shrugging: "They dumped your friend in the barrel to show you there's a time and a place for everything.

"Everybody always tries to blame all this stinky business on rotten old Potok over here," he said, "when it's that barrel I have to sit beside . . . with your friend's feet sticking out. . . . They should cut him open to let out all the gases. . . ."

"They should cut you open," I said. "But I suppose you could put it that way."

"No supposing. It's a sure thing. Like the intention and the intention behind the intention," Potok went on: "Only G dash D knows the difference, though it's as plain as the nose on my face. It's why I told them I could talk to you, you should listen to reason. You don't want to end up in a barrel someday like Big Mac?"

"Them?" I asked. "Who do you mean exactly?"

"SONNY BOY," Potok told me, though he was not much older than me, "being a character in the story of your life is no picnic. I really wouldn't mind a change of scene."

He laughed, like a groan, or a reproach. Other noises distracted me: the slopping of a wet mop, and the slap of footsteps on those dank stone stairs.

There was a distant jangle of keys followed by even louder concatenations of footsteps.

Presently, Inspector Larsen rattled the doors to my cell and instructed a young cop in the half light to let me out.

It took them quite a few minutes to find the key that turned the lock, and when the doors fell open I was told, "Please to come with us, please."

I climbed slowly, expecting firing squads.

"Remember what I told you," Potok called after me. "Friends come and go. The family is forever."

"You are looking at one of the few remaining lower middle class whites in Jamaica," Larsen explained. "He was detained a few years ago for speculating in foreign weapons and has never been able to clear himself. Nice enough fellow though," he went on, as if anticipating all my worst fears. "They say he was one of three Chaplains to the Somoza family of Nicaragua."

"He sounded more like pure Brooklyn to me," I said.

"Same thing," Larsen mumbled, as we climbed. "Once you get over that bridge it's all just about the same thing. In case you were wondering," he stopped himself in the darkness to add, "that wasn't your Mac in the barrel. Never mind who it was. A prop, if you like. Mac received decent Christian burial, and he even left behind a sort of political testament, for you, sir.

"I'm quoting," Larsen said: "Quote: the cruelty of our betters is only equalled by our snobbism in thinking we can emulate them. End quote. End Mac," Larsen said. "Lawd! You must be starving."

We were in the main vestibule near the constables' desk. Upstairs, no further indignities awaited me.

A steaming breakfast tray of eggs scrambled with ackee, salt cod, strong instant Blue Mountain coffee with sweet milk, bami cakes, and a Chinese egg roll was laid out on the very same table of the same room where Erskine had conducted his interview.

This certainly wasn't jail food. It had been brought in special for me. Delicious, too. I thought how all my West Side friends would be amused by stories of Carib-Chinese food in jail, if ever I was released. Meantime, Potok had it all wrong. I *was* getting the Class A treatment.

Or was this, perhaps, some sort of ritual last meal?

The door slammed loudly behind my back, like a gun shot. "Good afternoon, Professor."

Erskine sat down opposite me at table. "After a good lunch you will be escorted to Kingston. There you will be able to speak with your Consul as well as some of our Security people. Enjoy the meal. Care for a slice of pizza ?"

"My jaw hurts. . . ."

"Nasty bruise you got," said Erskine. "We'll have that looked after."

But it was hard to chew.

He said, "The violence was never meant to be personal. . . . Terribly sorry."

"Apologies accepted."

I must have been frowning.

He said, "I understand, Professor. You consider yourself a civilized man used to civilized treatment. You're angry, and frightened. Who are these barbarians? You ask yourself. . . ."

"I just think I have my rights," I said.

"O yes of course, those too . . ."

A loaded fork full of egg and fish now separated what I could see of Erskine's face from my mouth, and I thought of spattering him in his spic 'n span new uniform. Instead, I asked if somebody had bothered to inform Dyllis of my whereabouts.

"Miss Harrod's been told. She knows everything. She should be driving up even now to Kingston to see you."

That sounded too good to be true. Would I be released?

"Terribly sorry to say no," went Erskine. "The Prime Minister himself may wish to speak to you. It isn't every day our little tourist backwater catches a bonnyroo spy for itself."

"Just who might I be spying on," I asked, "in an abandoned motel with *Ms. Harwell*," I corrected him, "in Long Bay?"

"Tradecraft is tradecraft," Erskine said. I heard Larsen's crisp laugh. Then he was making apologies to his superior officer. Erskine said, "Your people use the word destabilize, I believe. At the moment our Government is very hard pressed for exchange to keep the support of the Jamaican people. Our resources are all, alas, nonrenewable. Busta's former blokes are making deals everywhere: with the aluminum people, even with Rastas. I'm afraid I can't say anything more about your case."

"My case?"

He nodded at me, grimly.

"You accuse me," I pressed on, "of being in the employ of certain revanchist elements of your own people. Am I correct?"

"In a manner of speaking," said the Brigadier. "It could be so. . . . As it were. . . ."

"Why?"

"Motivations are not my duty to explore with you, Professor. Nor are they Deputy Larsen's. A man is a complex mechanism like a watch. When the watch is broken you go to the watchmaker, not a policeman. I simply hope for your own sake you will be somewhat more cooperative with the various government officials you meet in Kingston town than you were with that silly-ass rabbi."

"Cooperative?" A certain leering suggestiveness both men were giving off puzzled me: My cooperation seemed to mean different things to different people. I was feeling confused.

"We are a fair-minded people, Professor," Deputy Larsen said. "We wish you no harm, but you'll have to see the watchmaker."

The Brigadier rose and added, "Good luck."

He waved in two more uniformed men who accompanied me to a waiting Land Rover which had already started to rev its motors.

6

KINGSTON SEEMS LARGE, spreading out across bulldozed hilltops, a city sort of like all the shabbier sections of L.A., with large areas that are so entirely shantified one thinks of Delhi, or Calcutta.

Such a lot of excavations everywhere. It looks like they dug for aluminum right in the suburbs.

Downtown is dark and gloomy, roofed over. Ferocious dogs bark at intruders in the new split-level estate tracts of the middle managers. Everywhere there are hoardings and billboards: for GOODYEAR RADIALS, DRAGON STOUT, BOVRIL, BRILLCREAM, ENO SALTS: for ROTHMANS, CAPORALS, GREEN STRIPES: nobody seems to have much money but everybody is selling: PHILLIPS STEREOS, potted meats, cars, flats, washer-driers, OXO, NESTLE, SINGER, BUNGE.

Goods are not abundant, the people are; Jamaica has a balance of payments problem: taunted by advertising, the poor pilfer from the rich who have stolen from them for centuries. There's a certain burning stink everywhere, too, a smokiness to the air: cook fires, perhaps, or garbage disposal.

There are also the large white museum-like villas of the well-to-do, trimmed with flamboyant and bougainvillea, and tall new hotels rising above the barren freeway overpasses, but they are all snared in smog. We went out along the waterfront toward Port Royal, where the air was clearer, then headed back in a suburban direction, as if lost, or trying to lose those who were following us. But we never went toward the government buildings in the center of town. Up a steep and somewhat hilly grading on which a cricket match was taking place, with the bowlers having to roll up an incline, we stalled, and then crawled our way along the rutted new road. A cluster of tallish hotels with gleaming white facades were surrounded by high fences of hurricane wire enclosing barren fields, as if under quarantine. We pulled up to the oldest-looking of these, the Sheraton, ferned-over, glassy, in brown woods, and stone; and my two guards led me in through the revolving doors.

In the potted palm lobby, where flashy ponces and other highbinders lounged about, we were joined by two rather well-dressed plainclothesmen: they wore Carib shirts, like their Prime Minister, with trim pockets at the waist, and they seemed cordial enough as they registered me for a suite of rooms on the ninth floor, and then escorted me toward a private elevator manned by a youth who wore jeans, a Rolling Stones tongue tee shirt, and a Marvin Gaye woolly cap.

I was feeling rather under-dressed, as well as sweaty.

As if sensing my discomfort, one of them said, "Your things are all in your rooms, sir. You can change and shower later."

"Nasty bruise you've got," said the other. He touched my forehead gently with his warm fingertips. "We'll get the house doctor to take a look-see."

They led me out of the elevator into a large airy suite, bedroom and sitting room, with terrace overlooking the pool. There were my suitcases lying open. They'd been carefully gone through; nothing looked much disturbed.

"We'll be a while," said Numero Uno. "Make yourself comfortable. Can I get you a Red Cap?"

He seemed to be the senior of the pair.

I asked him if this was going to be "a private party."

"The Government thought you might be more comfortable with such an informal arrangement," he said. "You're only going to be interviewed."

"Debriefed sir," explained the second.

I said, "I believe I already was."

"Not by our Mr. Pullman."

I asked what was so special about Pullman.

"He's been known to take a man's briefs off," Number One said, "and if you keep your spectacles in your back pocket that's what he calls hindsight."

They both laughed at Number One's joke until a knocking at the door to the room interrupted their conviviality.

"Devil," said Number One, still sniggering.

A long lean seersucker gentleman entered, and introduced himself with a courteous little bow: "Am I in the right room?"

"Sir . . ."

"This is Colonel Randall Pullman's suite," said the second fellow. "Did you hope to see him?"

"I've already spoken to Pullman," the seersucker man explained, with an accent that was not quite Yankee, though meant to sound as if it was. His face had a sallow tan; it was lightly pocked, like goatskin. He fished for his papers in his vest pocket: "I'm Gonsalves, the American Consul. May I be permitted to speak with the Professor alone?"

His overly deferential manner suggested ill temper suppressed. My spirits raced. At last I was being treated like a U.S. citizen.

"May I come in?" Gonsalves demanded of my guards.

He entered to their shrugs.

"I should really like to speak with Professor Harmon alone," he repeated then, and again they shrugged and went off into the bedroom, and closed the door, and turned on TV to a rerun of the "I Love Lucy" show.

I felt as if the Marines had come to rescue me from the Riffs.

Gonsalves said, "They always use this suite. We're probably being bugged. I should warn you about that." He sank into an easy chair and pulled on his trousers. "Even so it's better to request privacy," he said. "Puts them on notice, don't you know?"

Gonsalves was in his early thirties, of Puerto Rican, or Chicano, or perhaps Philippino ethnicity, but a generation removed from *arroz* and *frijoles*. Obviously part of our State Department's effort to create a new image in the Third World.

But there was something about him I didn't think I cared to trust; a man in his position who seemed more preoccupied with keeping the crease in his trousers than with looking at my bruised face would have to be a lightweight, if not also a spook.

"You do what you think is best, Mr. Gonsalves. This is all rather new to me, I'm afraid."

"Well," he said, still not noticing my bruise, "I'm glad to see you've not been treated too badly, but you understand there could be very serious charges brought against you."

"I suppose."

With great earnestness, he added, "Can you tell me what happened?"

I went over my various protestations of innocence, my ignorance of McAvoy's activities, my desire for sea and sun with Dyllis.

Afterwards Gonsalves said, "You got more than you bargained for, didn't you?"

He seemed so utterly earnest and profoundly callow, a yes-man, a cypher.

I said, "Next time I read one of those Air Jamaica ads I'll go to the Hamptons, or Cape Cod for my holiday."

"Have you got a lawyer?"

"In New York . . ."

"I can try to contact him for you," Gonsalves said, "perhaps he knows somebody here or in Florida."

I said, "I'd like to make bail, or else there should be formal charges brought. . . ."

"I wouldn't—"

"Nevertheless," I interrupted him, *"I would."*

"If you've nothing to hide why not talk to them?" he said.

"About what?"

Gonsalves took out a pad of paper and printed with a little gold pencil: "Be helpful. But say nothing about your past connections. . . ."

"I'm glad you didn't say cooperate," I scribbled back.

"Of course not. Just don't make too many waves for your friends. . . ."

After I had read it he took this paper out of my hand, put it into his mouth, and began to chew vigorously.

I took the pad away from him and wrote: "They already know I was in OSS."

Gonsalves shook his head. He was still chewing. Silently, he bade me to chew that one for him. Swallowing, he said, "Most unfortunate . . ."

The paper tasted like bad soy sauce and left a sticky feeling on my gums. It was hard to get down.

I swallowed, like a man having a stroke.

Gonsalves wet his lips and spoke out loud: "You have a very bad memory, don't you, Professor?"

"That was more than thirty years ago," I said. "What's to remember?"

"Correct." He swallowed another scrap of the detritus. "Miss Parnell may claim you and McAvoy were close."

"Harwell," I corrected him.

"Yes of course, but she may. . . ."

"She may, *or did?*"

He wouldn't answer.

I swallowed again to bring up some saliva: "Mac used to invite me to his parties . . . rather jolly they were."

"That's understandable, sir, as spies have more fun."

"Do they really?"

"Sometimes," Gonsalves said, "though you might have been a set-up. Did you meet Potok?"

"Why?"

"We never speculate at the Department of State," he said. "There are tensions between this government and ours. Potok sold Uzis and Galils. Good weapons. You can't hit the side of a barn with the Chinese AK-47.

"Anyway," he said, "it's a dangerous world. I'll talk to the Ambassador and see if we can't get you a proper lawyer." He stood up and shook out his trouser legs: "You'll hear from us, Professor."

"What about bail?"

"Just stay put awhile," Gonsalves said. "It's a fairly rough time for everybody, and you're lodged in the best hotel in Kingston. I recommend the key lime pie."

As he started for the door I heard Desi ring out, "Hi honey, I'm home!" His nasal yelp reminded me of a voice Gonsalves might even now be suppressing.

I said, "You're Cuban, aren't you?"

"Yes sir, *hombre.*" He seemed to have jammed his tall frame in the doorway. "My family came to the States in 1960," he explained. "But I've been with State ever since '66. We're

Serbo-Cubans, you see. My middle name's Jovanyvich."

"You've always served in the Caribbean?"

"Oh, no," he explained, "I've served in a lot of different places; Israel, Bolivia, Bulgaria, Portugal, and then . . ."

"Then?"

"The Far East." He winced but would be no more specific.

"I see."

"Be good to yourself, Professor," he told me: "Don't look a gift horse in the mouth."

I said, "You're . . ."

"Nosey people get bee stings," Gonsalves said. "Try the key lime pie."

7

Pullman finally arrived about 4:30. My guards left me alone until then. Mostly they watched various quiz shows on black history and pop music. I showered and shaved, and felt much fresher afterwards.

I won't go into any of my thinking. Mostly it was about Dyllis. Where the hell was she? What was she up to?

I stood on the terrace awhile and watched the bathers, thinking I might see her. A lot of the trim-looking black men around the Boomer Bar reminded me of McAvoy. Poor old Mac . . .

Pullman arrived with a large greasy brown bag full of patties which he distributed to my guards, keeping only one for himself. He was a rather portly fellow, middle-aged, with high cheek bones, oriental eyes, a high bronze coloring. Dressed very garishly, too, in a red, green, and black dashiki.

When he finally got around to me, he said, simply, "Pullman, Security."

"Upper or Lower Berth?" I demanded.

"You will be joking out your arse if you don't cooperate with me," he bellowed, suddenly copper-faced.

"Just what would you like?" I stared down at the bright azure pool below. "I can't confess to what I never did."

"BULL TOOKEY!" Pullman said. "*Fe* confession we go to

church. I am a mulatto man. A *cast*. Do you understand?"
I really didn't.
Pullman said, "Not white. Not black. Mulattos. Do you follow me, Professor?"
"Sort of . . ."
Pullman's slanty eyes grew large: "Someday the whole world will be just like me—and Mr. Manley—light, cocoa-colored."
"I very much hope so," I said. "But you're not light cocoa-colored."
"I should hope not indeed," went Pullman. "I'm of the Mocha Cast." His glance was benevolent, and his heavy lips pouted: "Tell me, Professor, how would you refer to a man with an eye in his arse?"
"A person of hindsight," I now replied, without much hesitation.
"Absolutely," went Pullman: "Then why does a smart man like you permit himself to engage in criminal activities for your government on this island?"
"I don't own it," I declared, "so it's not *my* government."
"*NOT ME! NOT ME!*" Pullman's voice was mocking: "Spoken like some Upper West Side New York analysand. The isle is full of spirits, Professor, I'm quoting Shakespeare of course. Have you never been fluttered?"
"I don't believe so," I said. "Please explain."
"Would you be willing to submit to polygraph?"
"Lie detector?"
"Of course. You would be asked about your government and our aluminium."
I told him I wasn't much interested in business.
"So you willingly submit to this box?"
"The box?"
"Flutter box," he said. "Don't they call it that at Langley?"

"Very possibly. I don't know."

Pullman smiled, as if genuinely amused by my show of reticence: "I shan't give you the privilege of lying to our machine. How's that? Be a waste of time," he said. "Perhaps I should get rough with you. . . ."

"Torture?" A sudden migraine. My lips felt dry and cracked.

Pullman said, "For a Professor you have such a lurid imagination."

He munched on his cold patty and studied me awhile. Then he found an emery board in the pocket of his dashiki and began to go over one of his nails.

At last he spoke again: "Do you fancy pussy?"

"Huh?"

"*Poosy, poosy,*" he crooned, like a man calling to his cat. "Do you fancy that?"

I was blushing I felt so embarrassed.

Pullman said, "*Poosy is nice . . . and soft . . . and sticky. . . .*"

"Cut that out!"

"*Puss Puss,*" he flapped juicy fat lips at me: "Here *puss*. . . ."

"Don't you think you're being slightly gross?"

"Gross?" He had a spot of grease on his face from the patty. "*Honores Causa,*" he said. "I have my honorary degree in spy detection. Only fancy: Gross . . . because I say *pussy-pussy*?"

He stepped closer to me and with sudden vehemence slapped me hard across the right cheek.

"Did you prefer that?"

The side of my face felt numb, then it burned.

"To put the matter plainly, Professor Harmon," he said, "if I am being gross it be because you are nothing but a little pussy worm. So I think you will find I can be cruel as well as sophisticated."

Again he swung, back-handed, at my other cheek.

There were tears again in my eyes. Pullman slumped onto

the sofa and covered his face with his hands: "Forgive me O God he know not what I be doing."

When he spoke next he appeared to wish me to believe he was contrite. "Now then Professor Robert Harmon we don't know why your Big Mac, of all people, tried to kill our Prime Minister. This is not the first time such things have happened. As you probably know, we are somewhat hard-pressed."

"I understand," I said, "I *used to sympathize.*"

Both sides of my face felt so very hot.

"Don't interrupt!" Pullman's face darkened. He looked blank and cruel, and then he softened again.

"People on this island are so *very, very* poor, as you may have observed. Most of us," he added, "are so *very, very* poor we have only holes in our underwear, if we had underwear to begin with...."

"I suppose...."

"The Manley Government has made a commitment to the poor of this island which is discomforting to some of those who are well-to-do."

"I know the line."

"Very good, Professor." He raised a hand to silence me again. Then Pullman reached into the pocket of his dashiki and removed a snap shot. He held it out toward me.

"Would you happen to know this man?"

The face I saw was dark, and thin, though not a black man's face. More likely, Levantine: Arabic, or Sephardic; Algerian, Moroccan, Syrian, *one of those* . . . .

He wore black horn-rimmed glasses and was very well groomed, like a Mafioso, or a TV anchorman: a dark silk shirt, a white silk cravat or foulard, in a windsor knot. Smiling at the camera, as if at some girl friend or fan, the lips were parted, the teeth capped, the grin poised, artificial.

I was sorry to say I had never been introduced to such a fellow.

"Are you sure?"

"I am telling you the truth. I wish I could be more helpful but . . . ."

"Very good, Professor." He seemed to mean it.

Pullman stood up again, and shook down his dashiki, and the flab underneath: he seemed bulky, huge.

"What does the name Norman L. Seixas mean to you?"

"Not much in particular," I said. "There was an American tennis player once, I think, with such a name. I believe it's of a Sephardic origin or derivation . . . that is to say, a Hebrew name of Levantine origins."

"Absolutely," went Pullman, "precisely." He seemed delighted with me: "A child of Israel . . ."

"As you say . . . ."

"But this is not the same E. Victor Seixas." Pullman waited me out a moment: "This is Mr. Norman L. Seixas. He is a *very, very* wealthy man. He is from one of our oldest plantation families. The family owned slaves. Until a few years ago he was our Justice Minister and . . . *by the way, did you know that*?"

'Can't say that I did.'

"I like you," Pullman said. "You have a way with words. "Can't say that I did." Only fancy," he said, "you have a way alright. *That Mr. Seixas is not important any longer is a function of the increasing sophistication of the Jamaican electorate. His party was simply voted out of power.* Additionally," Pullman went on, "his Agency affiliations are now well known to all of us down here."

"Ford or Chevrolet?"

"Cadillac," he said. "He is a covert op . . . . By the way, how was your lunch with Gonsalves?"

He chewed at me silently, and laughed.

Despite myself I was laughing with him.

"We may catch you yet at the other end," he grinned. "Where was I?"

"At Mr. Seixas. . . "

"Yes. Mr. Seixas has numerous interests on this and other islands. He is a charming and sophisticated gentleman, worldly, said to be an excellent host, or so I'm told, with a lovely and large plantation outside Savanna-la-Mar, and cultivations of sugar and allspice at Morant Bay, and coffee in the Blue Mountains. An important fellow, yes?"

"Very."

"Do you suppose you might care to visit with Mr. Norman L. Seixas awhile?"

"That's very flattering," I said, "but I don't see why . . . for what reasons?"

"You could talk about your mutual friend McAvoy."

"Not likely . . ."

"Why not?"

"Because I'm on vacation, and he's dead."

"How very rude of us," went Pullman.

Abruptly, he jammed a large hand inside his mouth, and with one swipe removed an upper and a lower bridge. Holding his dentures up to the light, he scraped some stuff off with his fingernail. Then he said, "Let this be a lesson to you, confidential agent Pullman. Always brush your teeth after sex"; and he replaced the bridge.

Smiling again, so that his expression now seemed slightly crooked, he wobbled his fat tongue about inside his mouth, and when everything seemed firm to his bite, said, "So you probably think I am a law unto myself in Jamaica. But now you just saw, through a simple and graphic demonstration, I am largely without teeth on this island. So now what do you have to say to me my friend? Can we play ball together, as you say: *be friends?*"

"I am not a friend of people who beat me up, and detain me against my will."

"Well put, Professor. You are not our friend because we believe you are on the wrong side, however, should you care to join the right side, I think you would find your treatment here *very* much better."

"I don't wish to be on either side," I protested.

"Quite impossible," Pullman said, "though valiantly put."

He wobbled those false teeth at me from behind with his tongue, and said, "Quick Professor: what's round like a pear, covered with hair, and every woman has one?"

"Don't know, Mr. Pullman-Bones sir."

"Oh be a sport," he said, "and I shall tell you." Pullman grinned: "It's a cunt, wot!"

"I wouldn't think so," I said, "and anyway why the riddle?"

"Because you are such an enigma to me, Professor, you really are."

"Because I'm innocent," I told him.

"Be that as it may, in plain or cypher, sir, you *are* an enigma. Did you know that?"

"You're flattering me."

"You could prove I'm not," Pullman quickly said. "You could telephone Mr. Seixas and try to see him, say you were close to Mac, as you call him, and, of course, he would insist upon acting as your host."

"And then?"

"We would give you something to put into his drink." Pullman whispered that sentence like a man who hopes he is being overheard. And, as if I hadn't caught his meaning, he added, in a louder whisper, "Something a little stronger than a sedative . . ."

"POISON?"

"Be quiet," went Pullman: "Do you wish these two dumb policemen to overhear?"

They were all laughing at my expression of shock and dismay.

Pullman said, "It will taste and smell just like Grand Marnier, or Cointreau, and just a tiny bit goes a *very* long way, I assure you."

"Nothing doing."

"Dear me fellows such a good natured person our Professor . . . ."

"I can't."

"Why not? The man Seixas is a murderer, an assassin, a clandestine mercenary of your CIA. He is planning to destroy our government. Ordinary people mean nothing to him."

"Then arrest him."

"No good," said Pullman, "as it would cause a scandal."

"And his death?"

"That must happen to all of us someday." He shrugged. "The venom is very difficult to trace. It simulates a stroke in some, heart attack, or palsy in others. You just pour a little into his rum punch when he's not looking and before a crow can flap his wings down he goes. Just like that. What do you say?"

"Then what?"

"Of course you will have the servants call a doctor, and he will be one of our men. Then you will go back to Kingston and be allowed to return to the States, having performed a truly important patriotic service for the new Jamaican state and its people."

I said, "Taking human life is evil. No matter what the cause. Why should I care to kill Seixas?"

"O very well," went Pullman, "just as you please."

He reached into his pocket a second time and produced another small pack of Polaroids.

8

They were all of Dyllis, naked: her legs apart, her mouth agape, upon a bed, encyclopedic as to postures and positions.

For indoor shots the color was rather good, I thought, no strobes. In one series of six, done with high speed Ektachrome D, sat upon the naked lap of Mr. Norman L. Seixas.

Shots of her taking him in the mouth, of semen flying against her fine auburn tresses like sprays of dogwood.

Another series showed Seixas entering her from behind, a mingling of ecstatic glances, and postures.

They seemed to be having such a nice time together.

One almost expected to hear the sounds of their pleasure as one flipped from picture to picture.

Back and forth, in, out, up, down, and sideways . . . I suppose I felt I wasn't sure who I wished to murder first: him then her or her then him?

Glancing at me closely, Pullman observed, "Those wide angle shots from the rear were done with the same type of Hasselblad camera used by your American astronauts in outer space. Tell me what you think of the definition?" he demanded. "They do seem rather spacey, don't they?"

The things a man will let himself look at: My hands were trembling with *their* passion. When I returned the photos to

Pullman he glanced over each one, appreciatively: "In case you need to know, they were taken late yesterday in your motel room at Long Bay before Mr. Seixas drove your lady friend to the airport in Montego. . . ."

"Montego?" Furious at being abandoned as well as betrayed, I said, "The truth is. . . ."

"Your Bajan lady was a yellow bird," he smirked. "She flew home on National. They knew each other quite a while, apparently."

"SO?"

"You would prefer to have your arse reamed out with a pineapple?" Pullman demanded.

A few minutes later we were sitting in a sullen stew of silence together. Our guards had been excused.

Pullman gave me a look of sympathy: "So perhaps our interests do converge . . . ."

"I don't like jealous people," I said, "and I myself am not a very jealous person."

He said, "All men are, Professor."

"Well, I can't stand being that way."

"Nobody likes it except old women," Pullman observed. "We have every reason to believe you are, at bottom, a decent sort, Professor."

I asked if that was meant to be a pun.

9

Pullman shuffled his fleshly photos like a deck of cards: 'It is not given to every man to serve the Tarot of history, Professor."

"Thanks a lot."

"You could be such an instrument."

He put a fatherly hand on my shoulder, and squeezed me gently. "Think about it."

"To kill my girl friend's lover?" I shrugged him off.

"To act like a man," Pullman said. "Mr. Seixas is a covert op of the American CIA. His class has been fucking all of us up the arse for centuries. He certainly plotted with McAvoy and your Miss Dyllis Honeywell."

"Harwell."

"The bitch," Pullman said, "wished to destroy our national movement. It is only just that they be destroyed by one who knows them, and has great anger against them, a former operative such as yourself, but *au fond* a decent sort."

"What sort of justice would that be?" I demanded.

Pullman started to deal himself a hand of tits-and-ass solitaire across his lap. I had to look away.

He said, "Professor, the sort of justice that exists at the moment is crude, admittedly, like a defective vibrator, but it can be brought off, to be sure. We do have interests in common, you and I. If they guess Seixas was murdered they shall not be able to prove very easily we were behind it. They will know. *So?* We wish them to know, and be warned. They cannot go about shooting at our party leaders. They tried *to kill* our Mr. Manley."

"But why me?"

"Because you sympathize with our cause as a humanitarian."

"Perhaps . . ."

"Moreover," said Pullman, "it is a fact that under the provisions of our gun court law you could be held in a detention center with Rastas and other pretty unpleasant fellows, indefinitely. I don't believe you would like that."

"Neither would my government," I observed. "I am a professor at a powerful American university . . . with tenure . . . ."

"Think it over, sir, you may have academic freedom in America, but *here*? Mr. Harmon," he added, "think about Seixas and your girl, your dolly, or, if you prefer, about the miserable life of our people, of protein deficiencies, rickets, and pellagra, on the one hand, and of flies that infect the eyes of our children . . . and a chronic dysentery. Of a soaring birthrate," he perorated, "hate for all things white . . . my own poor rotten toothless old mouth—*Harmon*—"

He was truly startling once he got started, but he stopped himself short again and apologized for "getting so carried away."

"There is also one other little thing," he said. "You will be very well paid."

"Money?"

"You must not be so naive," Pullman said. "Can you use

$100,000 in cash? You could buy yourself lots of other dollies with that. You could have your own house here. Think about that, too. And I shall see you again in a few minutes. It's time for my tea. *Toodeloo*."

10

T<small>HE WOOLLY-CAPPED</small> bellhop had appeared with a tray of tea things. One of my two plainclothesmen waiting in the hall tipped him with a note, and then spread the things out on the table.

Pullman explained, "I've some calls to make in the next room. You drink your tea and think it over. And drop that worried look, Professor. There's nothing in the tea. You'll have to add your own cream and sugar."

He went into the adjoining room.

My head was tilt full of dirty pictures; not so much a rush, as an engorgement and ejaculation. Gradually all that changed to dollars and cents. One hundred thousand greenbacks made even my jealousy seem worthwhile, for the moment.

So foggy-headed, I couldn't really think. But I saw little bright spots of rage before my eyes. I'd never killed any man close up in my life.

In France, once, with a silencer pistol, in the darkness, from nearly fifty feet away; and another time when we derailed that German train near Fürth, but we were half a mile away by the time the cars lay splintered on their side in flames. I never saw any of those dead German faces either.

Dyllis in bed with Seixas again came to me. *Up—down; wham—bam Bajan girl bye bye, and thank you ma'am. . . .*

She'd always looked so lovely in bed, I thought, lovelier than any place, so it would surely be a pleasure to watch the death paroxysms on Seixas' face and afterwards I'd get her alone in New York and. . . .

The trouble was I couldn't kill just because I felt like doing it; I was just not such a spontaneous or self-actualizing person; I was an intellectual; and it couldn't be solely for the money, or revenge, and Pullman must have sensed that in me: because he was asking me to commit myself to his cause. Depending on how deeply I felt about their right to control their own lives and destinies, he knew I would kill for him, and his people; to kill or not kill, for Jamaica.

I took no tea, but stood on the terrace and glanced down at the pool below. Some handsome dark couples were already seated around the little white tables, sipping expensive cocktails in the late high sun. Again I saw the drawn hungry looks of those people along the sides of the dusty roadways, and I thought I might kill to make that look vanish forever from this lush island.

When Pullman returned, he said, "Your ruminative face suggests we'll make a deal?"

"Deal?"

"Call it what you like," Pullman said. *"Ipso facto* . . . Polly want a cracker. . . ."

"Murder?"

"Be our friend," he said. *"Polly wally doodle all the day."*

His hulking jolliness suggested violence again.

I said, "You have a strange way of talking to your friends."

"That's because I really like you," he said. "Afterwards you will see how friendly all of us can be. You'll have the best *puss-puss* on the island, anything you like . . . ganja . . . cocaine . . . Chinese boys. We'll throw you a big party, too, how's that? A catered affair."

"I think you know why I will do this," I said.

Pullman was subdued, "I knew I was right about you, Professor. Even when I used to read your pieces in the *New York Review of Books* I thought here's a man with very good impulses . . . don't you know?"

I didn't quite understand if he was having me on again, or not, and asked, "How should I make the contact?"

"You will simply call on the phone, say you knew McAvoy, and that you'd like to have a chat, for old times' sake. I'll give you his number. Mr. Seixas will be most hospitable."

"Suppose he learns about my . . . er . . . detention?"

"He will, of course, he will, and he will sympathize. He'll want to learn what he can from you. For old times' sake. You will make chit chat about McAvoy, who is dead and, therefore, cannot say you are lying, when you tell Seixas he asked you to look him up if you ever came to Jamaica."

"Then?"

"You'll be on your own after that, I'm afraid," said Pullman. "Our venom will be delivered to the desk downstairs from one of the better shops in a costly-looking vial of essence. It may smell a little like Chanel, but will be odorless, and tasteless, too, when mixed with any other liquid. You will be followed all the way to Savanna-la-Mar, and beyond, in teams of two. *The Gleaner* will have printed the story of your detention, and release after questioning in connection with the attempted assassination of our Prime Minister in Spanish town two days ago, and you need not worry about your Ms. Dyllis. You can say you don't believe McAvoy did it. You're investigating your friend's death. Or you can say your girl friend abandoned you. She's being courted now by one of our Stateside agents, by the way. At this very moment they're getting ready for a long weekend in Nantucket."

"Will you kill her, too?"

"You worry about Seixas, " Pullman said. "That Bajan girl will be handled. We don't kill West Indian women when there are other ways. . . ."

"And suppose she gets a message through to Seixas about me? Or vice versa?"

"You can do it if you really try," Pullman said, purposely singsong. Excusing himself, he left with his two plainclothesmen, and that was the last I saw of him in Kingston.

Twenty minutes later the desk rang: my rental car was under the main *porte cochere,* the doorman had the keys, and a package had been delivered to the desk in my name.

11

THE ENVELOPE ON the seat of my car addressed to Professor Harmon said my "friends will be glad to hear from me anytime," and there was a Kingston phone number.

The tiny vial of expensively wrapped venom also bore a label: "Floral Musk: contents civit, magnolia blossom, essence of jasmine."

The smell was nostril clogging. One was advised to "use sparingly on the wrists and between the breasts for most alluring results."

I was sweating again, so I took a second shower and ordered from room service: a plate of curried barracuda, mango chutney, a Dragon Stout.

As I was finishing my meal Pullman called with Seixas' private number. If there was any trouble, he told me, I was to get in touch with a Mr. Barklay, a neighbor, with a large breadfruit plantation I could use as "safe house."

"Barklay's a regular sweetheart," he said. "You might consider staying with him overnight before you even pay your respects to our friend. He's charming, sympathetic, has a lovely old house, that was once a copra estate, and big breadfruits, *brambras,* big as your head. . . ."

I asked if he would be expecting me.

"O yes, bells and all, but I wouldn't go into too many details about things. He has his squeamish side."

Pullman was about to hang up. I'd forgotten to ask how I would be paid and took the trouble now to inquire.

"According to your just desserts, of course," Pullman said.

"I don't think I like your jokes anymore, Mr. Pullman."

"We thought you were a sympathizer," he said, "they don't work for the money."

"Well I do. . . ."

"Just testing, Professor," he said. "Just a tease. Having you on. The money will be delivered to your hotel suite immediately on your return, in small bills. Later the Prime Minister may wish to shake your hand.

"Will that be all?" he asked.

I croaked at him I thought so.

He wished me luck.

"Professor."

"Yes?"

"I like you," Pullman said. "Really I do, so be very careful. Enjoy yourself. It's not every day you do a man in. Have a little fun with it. Relax. Ready-aim-fire, that sort of thing. Nobody ever thinks he'll die so you'll have the edge on him: surprise. But first take in the scenery. Sav-la-Mar is not like Ochos or Montego. It's a bit of the old Jamaica . . . old legends of all sorts, you know."

I asked if he was absolutely certain Seixas would receive me.

"He will receive you, mon," said Pullman, "loud and clear."

12

WHEN I CALLED Seixas the phone rang a very long time. I felt giddy-nervous. The voice that finally picked up to answer was not that of any servant.

A broad Cambridge accent was "halloeing" me.

"Mr. Seixas please?"

"Speaking. Who may I ask is this?"

I gave my story so smoothly that I surprised even myself. Seixas received me equally smoothly: how sad about Mac; of course, any friend of Mac's was a friend of his; my *casa su casa,* just like safflower oil. He said he thought we should probably be a little cautious over the phone. Where was I staying? Could he call me back?

I told him my hotel, and room number. He said hang up. He would be getting back to me.

Half an hour later there was a knocking at my front door.

The gentleman on the other side of the door said he had come on orders from Mr. Norman L. Seixas to drive me down island to his estate for a late supper.

I explained through the transom that I had my own car and was planning to leave in the morning.

The voice said, "Open up *please,* Professor Harmon."

I fixed the chain latch and opened the door as far as a

generous wedge of cheddar on a rather small man with a perfectly round pie-shaped face and pecan eyes.

"Good afternoon. I am Carlos Almondero," he explained, "in the service of the Seixas family. Permit me to enter? You speak Spanish?"

"No."

He seemed harmless enough, no evident bulges in his clothing for guns, or things. But he gave off a smell of rusting metal, had an oily handshake, a Cosmoline smile.

Almondero headed straight for the bathroom and turned on all the faucets plus the shower. Steam began to billow around us when I joined him there.

"Guantanamero," he started to sing. *"Guajero Guantanamero . . ."*

Then he told me, "They gave you the best suite in the house."

I said, "I'm becoming rather damp."

He had long eyelashes and he batted them at me, coyly: "Mr. Seixas said I should not be too careful. He is a very important man." He had to shout a bit to be heard above the noisy gushing of all the water. "He is not in very good odor, at the moment, our Mr. Seixas. . . ."

"I'd heard there were problems," I said, wiping my brow with a towel.

Carlos Almondero said, "The telephones are not safe in Jamaica. These rooms, too. He said you should be visited to arrange for your coming to the farm. Are you all alone on the island?"

"Now I am. My girl was called home on an emergency."

"I bet you she was. It's a two-hour drive maybe more," he said. "I am instructed to accompany you now in your car."

"Very well." I improvised. "Let's dry off and I want to write a letter home. I'll meet you near the pool in half an hour."

"Very good." Again Almondero sang *Guantanamero* as he yanked off the faucets. Then he stuck his pinky up a spigot in the sink and a little black metal thing dropped into his hand.

"Damn bugs," he said. "They are every place even in the shower where a man must be alone to think, or sing, or make love to a woman. The police are so very suspicious of foreigners these days it don't matter. It was not like that under Mr. Seixas I tell you. . . . See. They've heard everything we had to say."

He wrenched on the faucets again. "We leave in one hour in your car."

He turned things off once more and dried himself down.

Stepping into the living room with me, he winked, and said, "See you tomorrow, Professor."

He headed into the hall.

13

I CHANGED MY MONEY from one pair of pants to another, and slipped the little vial of venom in my jacket pocket.

I tried calling Barklay but there wasn't any answer.

For some reason I thought I should write a good-bye letter to Dyllis: "Darling girl, I think you should know I am being quite well treated. It's all a case of mistaken identity.

"The police told me you'd left Jamaica. Can't blame you. Nevertheless . . .

"If all goes well I'll be leaving end of the week and will call when I hit New York. Have fun. Stay sweet. Sorry about our spoiled vacation. Don't say anything to our friends yet . . .we'll talk, Rob."

I was about to address the envelope when it occurred to me to add a footnote: "Believe I saw an old friend of yours briefly in Kingston; Seixas. Very rich they say, and handsome. Your type? He seemed generously endowed. . . ."

But it was like sticking my tongue out at ghosts.

Just before leaving the room I tried calling Barklay's number a second time.

A woman answered.

"Mr. Barklay please."

The voice was American; "This is Binny Barklay. If you wish to speak to my husband ask for his number."

"Yes. Please."

"This is not his number," she said: "Boys are his number."

"I'm very sorry to hear that."

"Alright Sorry," she said. "Whom shall I say this is?"

"A friend of Mr. Pullman's."

I heard some whispering, and then another English voice came to the phone: "Barklay here. Don't mind her . . . family spat."

"Hello. My name is Robert Harmon."

I'd hoped there would be some sound of recognition but all he said was, "What can I do for you, Harmon?"

"I called at the suggestion of Mr. Pullman."

"O yes?" But nothing more than that.

I went on, "I called earlier."

"Sorry. We must have been out riding. Mrs. Barklay, she likes horses. . . ."

I said, "I am driving down your way later in the evening to see your neighbor, Mr. Seixas. Pullman thought I should tell you that, if you didn't know it already."

"By all means," said Barklay. "If you need help do drop by."

"I probably shall." His welcome seemed rather too restrained.

I said, "Will it be alright with your wife?"

"My wife visits," he said. "She's American, too. You'll like her. We also have a weekend guest."

"I really don't want to put you out," I said, a little sharply.

Barklay said, "Binny used to be very tight with Errol Flynn."

"How interesting . . ."

"The movie actor," he explained: "She likes men."

"I know."

"Will you be coming alone?"

"More than likely not. Mr. Seixas has sent a servant to show me the way."

"I see? Man with a pie-shaped face?"

"Precisely . . . ."

"Well, I'm afraid that red carpet he's laying out for you may get just a little ensanguined. We'll be on the look-out."

But I felt as if I was choking.

"Now don't you worry," he put in. "You be a good fellow and trot along down there and if I don't hear from you I'll have some of my own boys drop by at the Seixas place. I'm sure it will all work out just fine."

"Suppose I never get there," I asked, "it's a long drive. . . ."

"Ah yes. Mr. Pullman said I was to remind you he'd left a special present in the glove compartment of your car."

"A present?"

"Nice talking to you," Barklay said. "Ever eat at Peter Lugar's place over in Brooklyn? Jolly good steak there . . . and sawdust. . . ."

He hung up.

Moments later there was a knock on my front door.

The voice of Carlos Almondero said, "Time, Professor. It's time."

14

All the way down in the elevator I kept telling myself I would never do this thing, and whenever I glanced at little Almondero he looked so very grim and determined I wondered if I really would not.

I thought I should just warn Seixas and then go on my way. Something about the way Almondero stared at me so bashfully made me believe his boss had already been warned.

We went out the hotel doors and toward the car, and Carlos said, "It is better you should drive so I ride—how you say it—shotgun."

"Is it going to be dangerous?" I asked.

"Don't worry," he told me, without bothering to explain why.

So the servant sat in the master's seat, and vice versa. In my linen jacket and dark slacks I whistled and steered and Carlos, in some worn old cotton ducks and a tropical shirt, next to me, remained very dark and silent. I got a scare once when we stopped for gas and he asked if I kept any credit cards in the glove compartment.

"I never use those cards," I shouted, with my hand over his, roughly, on the little button, so that he was forced to remove it; gave me a very odd look, halfway between a stare and an acknowledgement.

From then on I was forced to follow all of Carlos' directions scrupulously, as if to pay him some proper deference.

The roads were pretty good, clear of traffic.

Close to twilight we pulled up past the marketplace in Savannah-la-Mar, and out through the other part of town into the country again. There were numerous rice plantings and the land looked very flat, and wet, and green. The air so dark with afternoon rain. Almondero suggested we pull over until the storm had passed. It would only be a few minutes.

We parked alongside a grove of banyon trees. The rains came and washed their trunks sparkling jet black. Afterwards the sky wasn't very much lighter. Daylight was going fast. A road sign pointed toward NEGRIL.

We started climbing a little again, went through a crossroads store, a couple of shacks, and turned up a coral roadway about three miles until I saw the outcroppings of a large green-chimneyed roof, and then, as we rounded a grove of mango trees and coconut palms, the Seixas mansion emerged, like the superstructure of a great ship. It was so very, very large and in such good preservation, too fusty to be beautiful, but certainly grand: this big white house with bay windows. Turreted widow's walks in the Victorian style took up most of the third floor; and there were huge gabled gantries. On the ground floor lowly-built wings one story high had been added on, at each end, so that the entire structure resembled a swollen version of our White House.

So many verandahs, and Tibetan stone lions, sun dials, gazebos, arbors, and kitchen gardens presented themselves in coats of pristine white that I did not notice the eight small garage sheds, the tiny thatched-roofed tabby shacks made of crushed oyster shells, beyond the kitchen garden, the corrals, and barns stretching out toward a marshy flatland and the sea, until we had pulled up under the main entranceway, and then an after-image of this vast domain took hold on my consciousness. No exaggeration to say Seixas was wealthy; he was one of the lords of this Earth; and he had much to lose.

He was waiting for us on the verandah alongside the *porte cochère*. Silk shirt, silk scarf, white trousers, and espadrilles; his habit was intended to make him seem even darker than he really was, and very turned out, too: he held a cigarette in a long yellow meerschaum holder.

Binns, a butler in a white jacket, stood near by. Mr. Seixas wagged his little finger. Binns opened the door to my car. Was I to feel complimented, or merely impressed? Mr. Seixas came over to the car and shook my hand, and glanced at me, and suggested I allow Carlos to park. But I said I would do it myself. There were problems with the emergency brake.

"Good of you to recognize me," he said, "I guess you've seen the pictures. . . ."

"In *The Gleaner*," I said, "not too long ago."

"O yes?"

As I drove out through the other side of the *porte cochère*, I saw Seixas and Carlos putting their heads together as if to talk.

I placed the Mini between a large new canary yellow Rolls and wonderful old baby blue Hispano Suiza, in excellent condition. Before locking up, I checked out the glove compartment.

Good thing it was getting rather gloomy out. No pistol was yet visible but as I withdrew my hand the back of it brushed against ridged metal. Planted against a bracket in the top of the compartment was a small nickel-plated revolver, a dead weight.

It seemed heavy against my hand, had a small pearl handle. Loosened from its brackets, it fell snub-nosed, flat, upon my palm.

I started to slide it into my deepest pocket but thought better; I'd probably be searched.

I got out of the car again, and locked both doors.

As I was straightening up, Seixas and Carlos came toward me.

"Still too wet to walk about," said the master of the house, "though there's much to see I assure you, so why don't you and I just have a drink on the glass porch?"

"That will do me fine."

Seixas turned his handsome reptilian face, wrinkled almost black in the glare of the sunset, from off my windshield. He told Carlos, "We'll have drinks on the glass porch. Tell Bussy. Then you may go, Charles."

"Go?"

"Take some time off! Get yourself a woman, go to town, have some fun, my man."

Carlos seemed troubled by such a generous invitation: "Won't the Professor be wanting company on the drive back?"

"I should hope he will be staying over," Seixas announced.

My blood turned cold. I said, "I honestly don't think I can. . . ."

He seemed awfully disappointed: "Why not, Professor? You would be very welcome." Sensing my fear, he said to Carlos, "Check with me later, will you? I know some of our down-island hospitality will convince the Professor. Now go and have some fun."

I waved bye-bye to pie face. But he stopped himself again.

"You ride the clutch," Carlos told me. "You should never drive a shift car."

"I don't often do in the States."

"That I see," Carlos said, grinning at me so that he looked very much like this big red raspberry pie from which a slab had been scooped out where his gap teeth showed.

15

SEIXAS AND I SAT opposite to each other on the glass porch like a pair of elegant faggots playing at hubby and wife.

A low circular glass table in white bent wood separated us. The drinks were served in large silver tankards. A black maid in a white apron passed around little sandwiches of smoked fish, spiced pork, barbequed breadfruit wedges, and caviar.

I told myself I should warn him, give him the chance to save his own life, then found myself wondering when I'd have the opportunity to slip him some bye-bye juice.

And how would I go about it?

Watching Binns bow before his master every time he brought a drink or a condiment, I thought, he must hate this Mr. Seixas as I do.

But he didn't seem to; he seemed to fawn on his impeccable master; and that made me feel all the more shabby.

"These old places need a lot of care," Seixas was saying. "I have over thirty in help for the main house alone, usually, and nothing ever seems to get done. Nobody much around the old place today. Just look at that louvre. The pickneys are forever throwing rocks. . . ."

Two split glass window blades reminded me of bullet holes. I said, "Do you live here all the time?"

"I have a flat in Kingston, too, and a place in Morant Bay just like this, but when I'm not here I'm usually on my yacht."

He pointed toward the sea. I saw the smudgy black line of a jetty, and a long sleek white vessel at anchor. The late sun flashed orange, magenta, and black off the windows of its many cabins.

Seixas said, "This was a family place. I'm rather sentimental about things like that."

I tried to bring up what had happened to my friend Mac, but he went on. "My father and mother were great believers in the value of property. They were also great breeders. I have eight brothers and sisters and I'm the only one who has remained on island. The rest are flung to the far winds: Israel, New York, Montreal, Joburg, London, Paris, Rome, and Williamsburg, Mass., you name it. Mother was a MacShane, from the Jewish *schöne* for pretty. Scottish Jews they were, and very well off, though a bit dour. Most MacShanes have only one offspring. Mother, though, she was different. Believed in breeding and was a genuine breeder herself. She raised orchids, mother did, as a hobby."

"How interesting. Do you travel much?" I asked.

"Only when I have business." Seixas grinned: "Or there's pleasure afoot, which would have to mean most of the time these days, I'm afraid. Unless you include the yacht. Which remains pretty much stationary. I've visited all the neighboring islands at one time or another with my sister Linney. My brother Smith has a place in Barbados; 'Los Serranos,' we call it. Lovely place. Good people, too. I was in Andros only last week for a couple of days."

"Business or pleasure?"

Seixas ignored my question. He clapped his hands together for the servants. "I have a place in Kensington and an efficiency apartment in Miami Beach."

"*Efficiency?*" I must have seemed incredulous.

"I like to whip up an occasional chocolate mousse," he said, "and I always make my own breakfasts. . . . Costs me $600 a month at the Diplomat just for a room and a half but I have cooking privileges and it's North Miami, you know, practically Fort Lauderdale, a little more class . . . not so many *kikey* types. . . ."

Seixas checked me with his glance.

Then he wanted to know how I was enjoying my stay in Jamaica, despite all the recent inconveniences, and when I pretended to reply in the affirmative, he leaned far over the glass table, and glared up at me, from under those reptilian lids, and said, "Shall I tell you a secret about Jamaica, Professor?"

"Yes?"

"No I shan't," he said, withdrawing, as if he'd only been teasing.

The servant arrived with another round of drinks.

Seixas waited for him to depart again.

He asked, *"Redst Yiddish?"* I recognized that phrase from the war, though I really don't know any Yiddish. We Harmons were Unitarians, or Ethical Culturites, as mother was a Halle from Cleveland.

"Tant pis," went Seixas. "Down here we tend to think of all you white New Yorkers as Jews. There are so many, after all. In any event, my secret was," he cleared his throat dramatically, *"enjoy the sun, enjoy the sea,* but don't look too hard at anything or you'll get a bellyache worse than from eating green mangos."

"Quite." I hoped I sounded appropriately clipped.

"Quite," Seixas agreed with me.

At a loss for what to say next I again exclaimed on the grandeur of the old place.

"It's been in the family ever since the time of Captain Bligh," said Seixas. "We're very ancient to these islands. . . ."

"So you said."

"We're like the dust here. We belong. My ancestors preferred tropical fruits to the dates and figs of Jerusalem."

"Quite," I said again.

Seixas put another cigarette into his holder and squinted at me like a mechanic examining a nail hole in a tire. "When did you say you intended to poison me?" he asked, then, almost matter-of-factly.

"Wherever did you get *that* idea?" I tried to match his stare with my own.

"Come off it," he said. "I *had* your girl so they've got you poisoning me."

He had me stand up then and come very close, and he patted me down, all over, a frisking, first-rate job, too.

"You're clean enough," he said, at last. "No guns. But what's this?"

He was holding that little gift box of specially-prepared scent up to the light.

"It's a house gift for you," I told Seixas. "After-shave. Musk."

"Really. How nice." He put the stuff down on the glass table and scrutinized me, as if amused by the antics of a very large but stupid insect.

Seixas' poise, his good looks, and seemingly excellent state of preservation were hateful to me then.

Full of sun crinkles, his face said, "Nobody's good at keeping secrets in Jamaica, Harmon. . . ."

He was laughing: "Neither were Dyllis and I, I'm afraid. But she's a real beauty, you know, smashing. . . . Breasts like silk. *Silk,"* Seixas said. "The color of boysenberries in milk," he added, "or cream. . . ."

I just couldn't respond.

Seixas said, "You former OSS blokes are all alike. Cool as cucumbers."

He slammed his drink down on the table. "Did you see what a big one I've got? Bet you you don't have such a big one as that?"

It was as if a bone had stuck in his mind. His head actually seemed to gag on something and sputter. And I was supposed to be the jealous male. He seemed far worse off than me. Really strung out on Dyllis, as they say.

Seixas gave me an aggrieved stare: "What's the matter with you *anyway,* Professor? Don't you know I could easily have you killed? I'm talking to you about your girl," he said. "Didn't you happen to know that?"

The temper tantrums of the very, very rich interest me. Seixas acted as if he thought himself invulnerable. But he already knew about the poison, and there were servants everywhere. I had taken no gun with me.

He said, "I could even have Carlos do you and keep my own hands clean."

"You'd never get away with it," I said, just like in the movies.

But he seemed to be somewhere else, in a different film perhaps.

Suddenly he said, "She's such a cunt that woman . . . and she really knows how to hurt a man. Anyway . . ."

He stood up again. "I sometimes think I wouldn't mind dying here, without her. Being Chief-of-Station here is such a bore. This goddamn island is falling to pieces. Most of my friends left long ago."

"Then why stay?"

"I'm Chief," he said, "it's my duty." Reflecting on that a moment, he added, "I had you searched, and Carlos went through your car. It's clean. Now I'm wanted inside a moment. Suppose you take your fucking poison and get it ready for my drink. I'm sure we might have been able to talk business, you and I. I'm not afraid of you. *Never was.* . . . We probably have some friends in common in New York City."

He didn't seem to want to leave. He was babbling at me, almost incoherently. "Don't bluff me. You came to do me in. Do it and get it over with." Standing high above me he went on, "If I were you, the best time to use that stuff would be right now when I go inside to talk to cook about supper. But how would you get out of here? O yes, of course, the car. . . ."

Seixas seemed to have it all so clearly in his head that nothing had to be explained for my benefit. A raving man. "Well, the car is always possible, I suppose; you could make it, except, when all is said and done, I *am* a human being. Why kill me?" he was pleading. *"Why me Harmon? Why not Pullman?"*

"I'm not going to poison you, Mr. Seixas."

"O yes you are, I know you are."

"I don't want to. I won't have to."

He started to leave me sitting there on the porch but turned back again. "I know what I'll do. I won't bluff. I'll call Langley. I'll get the buggers who put you up to this. . . .

"You just wait," he added, and was gone.

A moment later the maid came out with another plate of sandwiches.

Once again I declined, though she was a very pretty woman.

When she left me I took that little gift box of venom and tossed it into some shrubs on the other side of the louvered porch.

Seixas reappeared. He sat down and took a sip from his drink.

The maid came to offer him a sandwich.

He said, "Get away from me, you slut."

He looked shaken. A sneer had curdled on his face. Seixas said, "Jamaican women have their brains between their legs."

"Come on," I told him. "Talk nice. We haven't got much time."

Another little sip, and then, smiling, "How long before I'm dead?"

My whole face turned on me, like yolks and whites when they are mixed with cream and separated with lemon juice.

"What did I tell you," Seixas said. He popped his fingers and grinned, "I knew you would never have the nerve. Cuckolds generally don't. . . ."

"I can't stay," I told him, "as I haven't any more time. I'm not bluffing."

"She was just a plaything to you," Seixas said, "and yet *she* liked you better than me, that bitch. . . ."

"I don't really care anymore."

"Then stay and show me your horns," Seixas said, "and I will show you mine. We'll go get Pullman together."

"I will be glad for you to see them," I said, "just so long as you understand. I didn't come here to kill you, and I don't wish to."

"You'd do anything for that bitch." Seixas said: "I know. . . . I'm not stupid, *not* just some pretty face."

He was grinning at me, almost lewdly, without so much as a by-your-leave.

Then he came close up to me again, with that handsome carefully groomed and composed, and yes, pretty, rich boy's face. How many Jamaican lives, I wondered, had gone into the expense of capping just those pearly white front teeth?

Seixas didn't let me say another thing. He spoke again as if his tongue issued from beneath the lids of his eyes. "If you're not one of ours, you're theirs. No two ways about it."

"So I've heard before," I said, "but in fact *I'm not*."

"Tosh," he said, *"and double tosh."* And suddenly he was

glum, and ruminative, again. "I'm sorry for what I had to do to you. Just couldn't be helped. . . ."

"Why?" Demanded of him softly enough. *"Why?"*

"We wanted you back," he said. "You had contacts. You couldn't be such a big middle class kid all your life."

"It *was* my life," I said. "Just to study things."

"Don't be so naive," Seixas told me. *"You're so naive!"*

That word, that phrase again: twice, the coldest feeling everywhere in my body.

Hate is the coldest feeling. Pity this man and spare him? Why? How? I wanted him dead.

Before he could utter another syllable. Before my mood changed again.

My hands seemed to move, without my willing them, toward the mouth of that profound inexorably-bred contempt.

Crikey; I wasn't bluffing.

Suddenly they were like large steel manacles about his throat, and though they felt mostly numb, the fingertips were like sensors once again, and an old ease with each long digit—a sort of sensitivity to the tips of my fingers—was uppermost in my mind as I felt for certain fine points in that soft nape of flesh, and squeezed.

Those eyes of Seixas became frog-like and glowing.

He was smaller than me by half a foot, so I had to lean far over him in a crouch to get proper leverage.

"I'll show you who is naive, old sport," I kept telling Seixas, "I'll show you. . . ."

It was just the way it had happened that time in training at OSS school with my army bunkmate, Kaplan; only now I was out of control completely, squeezing, and squeezing again, inexorably, harder and harder, so that he, at first, tried to resist me but really couldn't except to keep on blinking the eyes, quite rapidly, as if his ocular muscles alone could dispel my grip.

Seixas could hardly even utter a discernible sound. He made all these strange blithering noises, and wet my fingers with his spittle. My hands could feel him swallowing once, and then again.

He seemed about to gag, or puke up all his bile, and when I let up so he could at least catch his breath, a moment, he told me, "Dyllis and I, we came in sprays of apple blossoms, you sneaky little KGB bastard. . . ."

So then he kicked me in the shins hard and that really hurt, and I wasn't bluffing at all anymore as I began to squeeze again, and he commenced to spit flakes of blood across my knuckles, and again he gagged, and choked, and couldn't swallow, and seemed as if he might even come, but his knees began to bend and he fell backwards, smashing his head and shoulders, too, and then he was dead.

His last words were, "Pullman to Montego Bay."

Then he fell down heavily, prone against the flagstone porch: Seixas' body dropping made such a loud clatter; from all the change in his pockets, I supposed.

So *they* had me back alright. I had done Seixas to a bloody turn. But for whom?

16

THE GREAT SILENCE which followed from all the violence of this, my new knowledge, seemed as empty to me as all eternity.

On the floor of the glass porch, in the rapidly commencing twilight, I stood with besmeared hands above the body of my fallen adversary, and I was all atremble.

Takes one to know one, they say. Well, they'd figured me rightly, *whomever;* you never can forget that sort of training.

Seixas as corpse was perfectly rigid, groomed, composed again. His shirt tails hadn't even come out of his pants. Nor was his scarf undone. There was just a cultivated air of insouciance to the way he'd displayed himself in death, a slight pinkish froth of blood about his lips; his face seeming almost as blue as my net shirt.

I bent way over his body. A strong smell of blood mixing with all the brown rum reminded me to wipe the backs of my hands along his white ducks.

He had beshat his pants and when I dislodged him a little the smell was heavy, and feral.

I also found a tiny Uzi machine pistol in a holster strapped along the dead man's left calf.

I removed it and stuffed it under my jacket in my belt. Then I started toward the door that led away from the glass porch.

That whole house seemed emptied out. Lost in its luxurious vacancies I was like a noise with no sure direction in which to be diminished.

Abruptly, Binns emerged from behind a lacquered screen from Nepal. "Something I can do for you, sir?"

"Better see to your master on the glass porch."

I ran out the front doors toward the cars.

Somebody was screaming: *"Please wake up master, please. . . ."* The door jammed so that it took a while to pull open.

A little *ping*. It felt like a bee had stung me in the rear end. I'd been hit.

Alongside the car I searched for that Uzi which had gotten stuck on a piece of running board.

Another sharp sound, and broken glass rained down from the windshield onto my face.

I still couldn't believe it; killing Seixas, that simple, an agent of my country and now he was just another dead bloke.

Carlos fired a third time, and then I picked up the Uzi and squeezed a longish burst in the direction of the nearest Tibetan stone lion.

After a long silence came a voice I'd heard before, but where I knew not:

> *"O the night was dark and hazy*
> *when the piccadilly daisy. . . ."*

I fired two short bursts in the direction of the sound.

Then a child ran between our paths of fire. I found my keys, turned the lock, pulled open the door, lunged inside, shifted gears. The gears were—*where were they?* But the keys were in the dash. . . .

The motor turning over jerked me forward with my feet still out the door. I drove straight through the bushes in low until I hit sand and saw that I was on the roadway.

Then I sat straight up and started down the road in the direction of Savanna-la-Mar.

17

Passing by the little corner store in Tiddler's Bay, I parked and ran inside. Some loafers were listening to reggae on the juke. There were four or five of these boy-men doing a sort of dusty hustle in the sun; their heads under those woollen skullcaps faced the earth until they saw me coming at them on the run. Then their eyes grew big, and there were raspberry grins.

The whole backside of my trousers was bloody. But I wasn't feeling that much pain.

"You're hurt, mon," said one.

"My time of the month," I shouted back.

The female storekeeper, a dusty fat aunty in a stocking cap, said, "You'll be messing up my things, sir," but she also let me pass.

I found Barklay's number and dialed.

He answered right away, with a "heigh ho the wind and the rain."

"All done," I said. "I'm at the store in Tiddler's Bay and I'm bleeding."

"Be right down to fetch you," Barklay said. "Are you armed?"

I glanced at the Uzi which had become an extension to my right arm.

"I took a machine pistol from Seixas."

"Stay inside the store," Barklay said. "They'll be after you. Don't shoot anymore unless you have to. We don't want to start any riots. My foreman and I will be coming for you in the half-track."

When I hung up I felt faint.

The woman came from behind her counter, stared at me, hands on her hips.

"You *are* bleeding, sir."

"Sorry about that. I'm being picked up. I won't make too much of a mess."

I asked if she could fetch me a clean rag.

"Certainly sir, and something cool to drink. A ginger beer perhaps?"

"Just keep everybody away," I said, pointing with the Uzi wildly, "until I'm fetched. . . ."

The yellow Rolls sailed by, and then brakes squealed; it stopped, backed up. They must have noticed my car.

I wondered who could be driving, and tried to get a look around the corner of the telephone booth through its tinted windows.

Couldn't see anybody.

The Rolls accelerated and moved on again.

I began to feel pain, a sort of toothache of the buttock, throbbing, intense.

To keep myself from blacking out I was singing,

> *"Alle menschen werden bruder*
> *tochter aus Elyseum. . . ."*

Why that I don't really know.

> *"Alle menschen. . . ."*

And then:

> *"It's Saturday night and I just got paid*
> *Fool about my money I wanta*
> *   get laid:*
> *We're gonna rock tonight*
> *We're gonna roll tonight*
> *We're gonna rock and roll*
> *   tonight. . . ."*

There was a sudden vast, great grinding of gears, and then this amphibious half-track appeared, painted sky blue all over. A whiskered face jutted out of the well. "PROFESSOR . . . PROFESSOR HARMON ARE YOU THERE?"

The boys outside were pointing.

"In the store, Barklay."

The juke box blared a new tune. "God help all of us," aunty cried out, "Have mercy. . . ."

"It's safe, sir. You can come out now," said that fair whiskered face.

"Come in and get me, you and your man, with your hands up."

"See here, we certainly don't mean you any harm," said Barklay.

"Prove it."

I waited a second, then said, "Now come on in with your hands up, you and your man."

A clammering of feet on cast iron, and then they both appeared in the doorway: this well-built black fellow, armed with shotgun and machete, and Barklay, pistol in hand.

He seemed so very slim and red-faced under his large grey mustache.

"Drop your guns," I told them. "Keep your hands high."

"Now see here my man. . . ."

"I'm not your man, I'm bleeding. *Schnell.*"

I heard their weapons clatter to the ground. Then I came out. Barklay exclaimed, "You're hurt!"

"Give the woman a few quid for the mess I've made," I told him. "Then help me into your half-track. Ask those lugs to carry your weapons."

He snapped to, like an eager subaltern.

When I threw my arms about both their shoulders and started limping toward the car, that Rolls reappeared, maybe five hundred feet away.

"Down on the ground!" I shouted.

Falling face first into the dirt I felt this terrible stab of pain. Almost lost my breath. They all fell next to me. The Rolls—its 8-track stereo playing *Guantanamero*—moved by very slowly as if on patrol, but was unable to see any of our prone bodies behind the half-track.

Afterwards they all helped me up again and I had to be lifted feet first through the hatch of the vehicle whereupon I blacked out.

18

I MUST HAVE BEEN dreaming. I was talking to a representative of Plants Liberation, a very red-faced man—like a tomato—who said things such as, "Scraping a carrot is an act of barbarous cruelty."

Then Seixas intervened and began to defend the Agency. It didn't interfere with people's lives. It was good for people, like a parent.

The Plant man said, "On the cultural level that's rather like willing yourself not to think of a large red rooster."

Seixas had three large holes in his head; he looked rather like an eggplant prepared for stuffing.

He said, "You mustn't expect too much of our race. We're all pretty rotten, you know. I was once a rogue elephant. Without moral sense, or respect for the law. Only now I am plainly just dead."

He lay down in a grave and I saw a big worm poke out from one of the holes in his forehead.

"Sorry to have *disinformed* you about my condition, Harmon," he said, "but you probably should have known better. The news media have given us a sinister vocabulary that never, in fact, existed in the real world."

Waking face down on satiny sheets, in a high canopied bed, I felt somebody dab at my sore rear end. A woman's voice said, "Nothing sinister here, sir. Just a swab. Try to relax. . . ."

I was in love with that voice, even though I couldn't turn around to see the woman.

My eyes were open and, after awhile, I saw Barklay sitting in the throne chair next to my night table; it looked rather like a potty.

He swallowed at a bit of whisker and said, "Quite a time you had yesterday. Feeling any better?"

"O quite. It's morning?"

"Quite," said Barklay. "You needed your rest. That bullet passed right through your fleshy part, thank goodness. . . . No possibility of any serious harm, only an inconvenience, I'll warrant you. Best you rest." His smile was soothing: "Let Marina see to your nursing."

"Thank you, nurse."

"Very good, sir."

She dabbed at me again.

Barklay was saying, "Quite a story in the *Gleaner* this morning about my neighbor."

I felt a little panicky. I hadn't been dreaming all along. I had really killed Seixas. Now what? I must be a wanted man.

"I'm to get you a lawyer," Barklay said. "I've already spoken to Pullman."

"I don't need a lawyer. I want to get out of Jamaica."

"Easy man," he said. "That's quite impossible at the moment. You're going to have to stand trial and, perhaps, even be sentenced. But I think we can prove it was justifiable homicide."

Then he explained all about the pictures of Dyllis and Seixas: I'd been in a jealous rage; I'd tracked Seixas down to confront him for an explanation, and there'd been a fight. I'd shot him.

"I strangled him," I said.

"It said shot twice in the *Gleaner*," Barklay corrected me.
"Christ..."

"So," Barklay said, "we'll have supper together and talk some more." Turning over was painful to me; he had a captive audience.

He said, "You'll see. It will all work out. Cheer up man. Nothing to get that worked up about. Piece of cake...."

When he left me Marina went with him; they didn't seem to be going in the same direction.

I dozed, and woke, and dozed off again.

It was dark outside my windows when I woke again; a servant moved about the room, setting a bridge table for supper.

Marina appeared at my side, and when I saw her she was beautiful and dusky, with heart-shaped lips, this mulatto woman of no more than twenty-five, in her tight white nursing habit, the little three-cornered cap stuck primly to her head like a sail. So fastidious; a Johnson & Johnson ad.

She changed my dressing, and then helped me out of bed, set me down in an easy chair with a foam rubber donut cushion.

I said, "Do you know who Johnson & Johnson are?"

She grinned, "I know what a Johnson be."

I said, "Johnson & Johnson, sweetie."

"Two of them," Marina said. "That's funny."

She had only one other thing aside from tenderness on her mind, and I was *hors de combat*.

"Who will be at dinner?" I demanded.

Marina said she didn't know, but she was to ask on behalf of Mr. Barklay if I preferred whisky or ganja for my sundowner.

I said nothing at all, because I thought I wanted to be alone.

Marina was tittering as she left the room.

I couldn't be cross with her. Just myself. Something in

dreams had penetrated to my consciousness: that I had been the set-up, the singleton, as it were, patsy first, last and always, all along. I was Pullman's boy, his baby; he was my control; and none of this was being done for Jamaica, but for the Agency once again. I'd killed for the same old masters as before. Pullman was just a double. Only *he* could have told Seixas I was bringing along venom. . . .

After such knowledge, what behavior? I was wanted for murder, and I would have to stand trial in an unfriendly country. Who were my allies? My *enemies* . . . I was the guest of Pullman's foremost accomplice, Barklay, I reasoned. He would most probably have to be an Agency person, too. Perforce.

Why had Pullman wanted Seixas out of the way? To promote himself, I thought; he would now be Chief-of-Station. It was that simple, a matter of greed. But I was much too shaken and frightened to regard this news calmly, to reason through every new detail. I knew my life was in danger from these so-called officials of the Jamaican people. If I wasn't very, very careful, I'd be dead by morning.

The miracle was I was still alive. They must be wanting the trial very badly, I thought. They must need the trial. . . .

To smear the past and cover the future. They'll do me afterwards, I decided, if I'm able to survive dinner.

Barklay knocked on my door discreetly before entering. I asked him, "Why have you waited so long?"

19

"Dear fellow..."

"Why not get it over with right now?"

"Don't give it another thought," he said. "You're doing just fine. You looked like something the cat dragged in last night but now you're up and fresh as a daisy and supper will be only a little while longer."

He had a drink in one hand, wore a blazer with some kind of gold and silver university crest, an open shirt; had even waxed up his mustaches.

"We've all decided you ought not to have any intoxicants until you've gotten some food into your stomach," Barklay said. "Bad on an empty mess tin, you understand."

He seemed a little high himself. Opposite to me at the well-set bridge table, he seemed, by his peevish glances, to be wondering what exactly must I be thinking?

I didn't let him guess forever.

"Will Pullman be paying me another visit?"

"Not likely," Barklay said. "I do the baby sitting. Tomorrow morning you'll go up to Kingston; bail has been arranged. You'll see a lawyer, hopefully Pullman, too. There's even a chance you might get to see the British and American Ambassadors. In concert."

"I want to see Pullman. I must see Pullman," I said.

"Just a sec . . ."

"I want Pullman," I said.

"Frankly Professor," he said, "you're not important enough. . . ."

"Important?"

"Is your name Frank Plac or Henry Beans, or Farrah Fawcett-Majors?"

"Certainly not."

"Then you're not one of the important people of the international set, are you?"

Ignoring my face: "You know, the local people aren't very sophisticated. To them you're rather a hero. The locals . . . One of them goes berserk with his machete, and the *Gleaner* reports: RUNAWAY BAY MAN CHOPS 8. So when a highly respected American visitor with academic credentials shoots two or three holes in the head of our former Justice Minister (and he being from one of the wealthiest and oldest families on the island) and the motive is sexual jealousy, male competitiveness, or what have you, even when it turns out to be strangulation, our people down here they just eat that up."

"Then I am important. . . ."

"To the primitive mind, yes," Barklay answered. "But. . ."

"*I am not* a sexually jealous person," I interrupted him, then, with a shudder. "I saw a psychiatrist for twenty years to get over that. Had a lot to do with my mother. The way I was brought up, you see."

He was laughing at me, as if I was some sort of clown. "Psychiatry? What do they know of psychoanalysis down here in Jamaica? Besides, old boy, it doesn't really matter what you are, and who your mother was. *It's what these people would like to think you are.* I hear there's already a song in the marketplace in Kingston:

> *Mr. Seixas go bang bang*
> *Professor Harmon go bang bang. . . ."*

"Marvelous. Wait till my friends in New York hear that one."

"O, they'll refine it a bit before they cut the record. But it will make the charts, I assure you."

"That's another reason why I'd like to see Pullman *here*," I stressed, "before going up to Kingston."

"I've already told you that would be quite impossible."

"I think not."

Barklay went grrrre, so that his mustache vibrated. "Now don't make me angry. We'll have a nice dinner and a smoke and I'll have a lovely after-dinner treat for you."

"In my condition?"

"Jamaican women *fe* sure know how to accommodate," Barklay said. "Be sure of that. The woman I'm thinking of, she had a husband who lost his legs in a cane-cutting contest. Well, one can get used to certain types of accommodations," Barklay pointed out.

"How nice. But when can I see Pullman?" I asked again so as not to let him off the hook; then a servant appeared with a tureen of green turtle soup, and as he began to ladle out some of its fatty dark froth into both our plates, Barklay ordered sherry. Then he said, "Why do you need to see him?"

"Who?" I was distracted.

"Pullman. You keep saying you must see Pullman."

"Because I have certain questions needing to be answered."

"Just don't trouble your head with thinking right now," he said. "It's probably bad for you."

"No trouble at all," I said. "It's probably what's keeping me alive. . . ."

"You think so?" He laughed at me and broke some bread, showering the crumbs across the cloth: "Ridiculous."

I waited for him to start spooning soup before I would take some myself.

20

The rest of our dinner together went smoothly enough, I suppose. It was really quite delicious; some sort of potted fowl, or rabbit, in a sweet curry sauce, with coriander and currants, and cassava mash, and wonderful small bright red tomatoes—surprises inside the mouth.

Seized by the greedy hand of my hunger, I permitted myself not to speak of Pullman through all the main course. Barklay knew I knew he knew, and so must Pullman, by now, I assumed. So very civilized; the lions lying down with the lambs.

Over the sweet custard, Barklay told me of his childhood and schooling in Ireland. His parents were retired civil servants. He'd gone to a series of just barely adequate Catholic boarding schools run by the Christophers, and finally ran off to sea in the British Merchant Navy just before the Korean War. He'd had a knack for the sea, received one promotion after the next, and was finally made master of a small cargo tramp that plied between Kingston and Tampico. Then troubles started. He'd lost his boat, had to choose early retirement; he didn't want to go into any details except to say he'd been wronged, it wasn't his fault; he'd been entirely wronged. He'd come to Jamaica and bought land some fifteen years ago, and now here he still was.

He said, "I was considered very handsome in my youth . . . ."

No comment from me.

Then he said, "It wasn't anything illegal, drugs or stuff of that sort. That came later. . . . It was a . . . sort of a . . . moral problem I had. . . ."

"*Boys?*"

Barklay quickly spooned himself more custard. His tongue flicked out at the golden yellow mess on his spoon. He grinned, and asked, almost casually, if I had ever experienced "utter inexorable bliss?"

"I suppose so . . . ."

"You wouldn't say it that way, if you really had," he went.

I wasn't sure what he had in mind. He seemed to be asking more of me than a memory. I thought of Dyllis and of losing consciousness with her. I didn't want that to happen *now*, with *anybody*.

"Still, you're a good sturdy chap," he said, "I can see that. Judge not that ye be not judged. . . ."

"If you say so," I told him.

He said, "I'll have Marina turn down your counterpane," and clapped his hands three times.

She appeared with coffee and cups, and while she helped me back to bed, Barklay poured some for himself and drank.

He said, "In Scotland they give you a dog, instead of a hot water bottle, when you visit certain castles. Here, in Sav-la-Mar, we have our Marinas. Now my luv," he said to her, "do you suppose you could be a pet for the Professor?"

"No trouble, sir," she said, "you wants me to bark, too?"

"That won't be necessary."

"O yes, sir, I tink so," she said, and barked loudly twice, and then she made a yelping, squealing sort of noise, and a purring, more like a pussycat.

"I'll turn the other way," Barklay said, and when he did she removed her nursing whites, and crawled naked into bed beside me.

I caught a glimpse of her heavy torso and strong brown legs, and there was an odor like roasting almonds that suffused my nostrils; she curled next to me and her skin was very smooth except for her buttocks which were pebbly, with chilblains, I thought.

Marina had reached out to me almost like a mother to her child. Her body was friendly, easy to get along with, accommodating; though I was not feeling aroused. She said, "O sir just relax, and I'll give you de Japanese backrub, later. . . ."

"That's a fellow," Barklay said, turning his back to us again, "she's just being friendly, our Miss Marina. You've nothing to fear from her. She'll keep you warm and cozy the whole night through and if you get too spooky she'll talk to you and hold your hand, or something else, now isn't that so Marina?"

She yelped and barked again.

I said, "Cut it out luv, you're a woman."

"O tank you, sir . . . tank you tank you."

"Company for the night," said Barklay. "You'll find she's very easy to please. Just twiddle her clit gently occasionally and talk nice to her as you're now doing."

"You're leaving me?" My alarm when he started for the door must have been on account of Marina.

Barklay observed, "You look like you have your hands full. Good-bye, for now."

Alone with this beautiful female I hardly knew, I thought of explaining myself. I certainly didn't want to hurt her feelings; I wasn't like Mr. Barklay and all the others, *whoever they were;* I was just feeling very angry at all women, because of Dyllis, furious for having been set up . . . .

"If I don't see Mr. Pullman in person down here by tomorrow morning," I had shouted at Barklay before he went, "you won't be able to drag me up to Kingston. You'll have to kill me right here and now, which could prove an unnecessary embarrassment to you and all your plans. . . . Pullman to Montego Bay and all . . . ."

But now with Marina I was feeling intimidated by such an abundance, so much easy warmth, an almost maternal understanding.

Even though I'm a man of fifty, there are times I still feel I need mothering. Just to be cuddled, you know.

Barklay had left me saying, "Stop all this talk about dying and get some rest."

Now Marina sat up in bed and trotted her little white cotton underpants off the carpet and pulled them over her backside again. "You won't mind sir? Be a little less indecent dat way. Since you don' seem to want me anyway like dat."

I said she was free to do as she liked. Afterwards, we cuddled like yams next to coals.

For quite some time we just lay like that. Inert.

But I couldn't sleep. Asked, "Why do you allow them to degrade you, Marina?"

"Allow?" She cuddled closer. "I've children, sir, dey like to eat, and me mother does de taking care. I've no wish to starve her, or myself, too."

She seemed so young I asked how many children could there be.

"I got five."

"Five?"

"No botha sir. Dey don' botha you no more den two or tree. Dey just costs more."

"You look like such a child-woman yourself."

"Two's my sisters," Marina explained: "Anais, and Rhyss who we called Asohita. Don't ask me why. . . ."

I asked if it was nice being a mother.

"A worry," she said, "but you get to be taken seriously. Even de Government got to do dat now. . . ."

She laughed. "I never wanted it like dis. I had a husband and he be . . ."

"Killed?"

"Dead," she said. "Chopped. Makes me sad to talk about dat. Why you want to hear all bout dat sad fretful stuff anyway?"

I explained, "It means I'm getting to know you a little."

"You like me?" she asked. "I like you. . . . Be enough . . . ."

"I'm grateful to you," I said, "although in no condition to have a relationship with a woman."

Again she sat straight up in bed, pulling the counterpane across her large breasts. Crossly: *"When you talk like dat makes me angry. . . ."*

"Angry?"

"You got no call," Marina said. "I do me work and dey pay for de tings. It is better sometimes, and other times worse."

She sounded like an Irish washerwoman; there's a little taint of the Gaelic to Creole.

Marina seemed very cross with me, but I wasn't sure why.

"Did I ask a bad question?"

"Sure because you say de wrong tings. I don' want your fucking gratitude. We can't eat dat and it don' put us to sleep nights."

"Sorry . . ."

Her breasts heaved against the counterpane. "You tink I minded de dog? I mind for sure all de *woof woof woof,* but when I leave here I don't even tink of such tings! Never. I tink of my happiness, and all de good does me for to be eating every day de week."

"I understand."

"No you don't," she said. "Dis life we hate, but we don' hate you one by one. All de time hating we don't, and cannot. Der be other things to do. I take night courses, Tuesday–Thursdays, to be a real nurse para-medical. Here money's better den in de whole of Kingston hospitals. Still I tink I would go dere someday, too, find de proper husband again. You savvy me?"

"I understand."

"You tink I want de Woman's Lib? All my life I got de Woman's Lib," Marina said, "since Jerome got chopped. Maybe before. We are born dat way down here, sir, and I am a woman, you see, and a caste, what I want I get for myself, even a good man, I tink. . . ."

I said I was glad she was so ambitious for herself.

"Did you tink I want to be de dog all my life?" Marina said, "I have five small ones. I am a woman *fe* sure . . . let me give you back rub . . . ."

"For sure," I echoed her.

"You doing OK," she said. "No botha. You could be a nice man. A woman knows . . . easy to see dat."

She bent over me and kissed my shoulder and neck, nuzzled at my ear. "You like dat, don't you?"

Despite my worst fears, there was growing evidence it felt good.

"You ever do this for Barklay, too?"

"*Fe why*? He be queer. Dat one can't raise it on him, never would try. But Mr. Barklay like to have his forehead rubbed with palm nut oil. De mon got headaches. . . ."

I asked Marina if she would allow me to offer her money.

"A tip?" she was laughing. "You got a great big tip for me?"

Clinging to my legs with her hands, she inched her way down along my body with kisses and caresses, with her lips, and her cheeks, and her fingertips, too, and when she came to the point of all those mounting indications, Marina took me into her mouth, and released me, and took me in her mouth again.

"It got an awful big swayback like some old mule."

She went down on me another time.

Then said, "Used to do dis for Mr. Dick Tiger, middleweight champion. That was one big Nigerian fella . . . ."

"I saw him fight. He was good."

"Didn't make no fusses like you," she said. "Most people don't you know."

I told her I didn't want to have to apologize to her again.

"*Fe* why? You must be a good man," she said, "because you was situated to kill our Mr. Seixas, and he and his class dey walk all over people. So you must be some fine fellow, I believe, even though he took your lady . . . de people say dat was right and just."

My feelings of gratitude had again put me on my guard.

Marina said, "Seixas wanted to take Mr. Manley's place, you know. He is one handsome man, our Mr. Manley, and I would do dis for him, too, but he has any woman he desires. All de time. He has a beautiful wife and chillins too. . . ."

Mrs. Manley *was* beautiful, from her pictures, I recalled.

"You're quite beautiful, too, Marina."

"Great big bloke you got dere. Crooked. I never seen one with de swayback . . . ."

She was encircling me again with those wonderful soft lips.

Can't remember much of what happened afterwards. All the

lights suddenly went out, and it was dark and very warm beneath Marina's body.

Bathing in all my most pleasurable feelings, I felt myself giving out to her, suddenly.

When I went off alone into all that scented nowhere, by myself, Marina cajoled me, as if I were her very own little baby: "Mustn't waste a drop. We'll take every little string to make de custard pie, and den we'll lickitde clean and put it back to de bed again."

21

Sudden glare on my eyes brought me awake.

Deep beneath our counterpane Marina huddled so that I could feel her breathing on my legs.

Pullman's great hulk blotting out most of the doorway.

Pointing at the lump in my bed: "You got de tumor, Professor?"

"Do you want my professional opinion Pullman?"

I was just glad to see that sly grinning fat brown man. Those wobbling candy dentures indicated he was in a somewhat quizzical, ruminative mood toward me.

"How's business?" I asked Pullman: "How's tricks? Dirty tricks?"

His face went dark. He shouted toward the lump in my bed in rapid Creole.

Pulling herself up in a hurry, Marina ran naked from my room, dragging one of the sheets with her like a wedding train.

"Fucking Mr. Pullman," she said, "nothing but de scolding . . . . Mr. Pullman he gives you . . . . Dat ain't no stationmaster. Dat's bad stuff . . . ."

"She'll get over that," Pullman explained, with a shrug, "she always does. We're old old friends actually, but I will never marry her unless the life she must live on earth to earn her daily bread changes."

This early in the morning I hadn't expected any confessions. What time was it?

"It's not quite 4:00 A.M." Pullman said, "You sent for me?"

"I guess I have regards for you from all the boys at Langley."

I held my breath.

His face went glum; he didn't even seem that cross with me. He went over to the sideboard and poured out two cups of lukewarm coffee, and brought them over to the night table alongside my bed. Then, like a doctor, he placed a flat smooth warmish hand on my forehead. "No fever . . . very good . . . means there is no infection. It's the vibramycin. Very *avant garde.*"

Pullman backed away from me to the throne chair next to my bed. "Now then, Robert, since you wished to see me and I have made a special trip down here, perhaps we ought to talk about our little business together. It's very late."

"I don't want to stand trial. I don't like the whole business of a trial."

Pullman chuckled, easily, softly, like an indulgent parent. "It's for your own protection, Robert. You know as well as I it wouldn't do to go back to America and have people thinking you were an agent. Your colleagues, old Blake, for example, it would never wash with them.

"We also have our own internal necessities to be thinking about," he added. "A good clear trial at which Seixas and his gang could be exposed as agents is risky, so we shall settle for 'philandering decadence' and you as his justified executioner—that will suit us nicely, I believe, for the moment—a truly Jamaican solution for the women voters, and there are more of them than men down here."

I stared at Pullman like an accuser. "I imagine that would also suit your needs. Pullman to Montego Bay," I added. "ALL ABOARD. . . ."

He grinned.

"What did you expect? Why not *mon*?" My accusations didn't seem to surprise him. "I don't get your problem."

"You set me up. You and Seixas worked together. To protect you own cover he had to be out of the way. Maybe you think you'll be the new Chief-of-Station. I don't know . . . ."

"Station Master," he corrected me.

Pullman took a big noisy sip of coffee.

"Very astute. But crazy, Robert. I always knew you was one smart nut."

"It just came to me," I said, "Seixas had to learn from somebody about the poison and you were the only one who knew."

Pullman said, "Don't you know I could kill you because *it just came to* you?"

"I'm afraid you'd really have some explaining to do then."

"Maybe so, but who knows? *Fe* sure! You were like a mad dog after your visit to Seixas. We have all the witnesses at Aunty's store, and maybe we say how you attacked an officer of the Security Service. I bet you Gonsalves from the Consulate will fall for that one, *fe* sure, and it would get no further."

I said, "Because he works for the Company, too."

"What's a smart bloke like you doing as my prisoner?" asked Pullman, stiffly. He sat upright, sipped more coffee. "Yours will get cold."

I didn't care for any coffee. Caffeine makes my mind race and it was going fast enough, thank you.

Pullman said, "You think I am CIA?"

I didn't feel I needed to repeat the accusation.

"You got brains, Professor, only dey been a little bit scrambled up with eggs." He grinned at me, and touched my arm, softly. "But you are right about thinking in terms of doubles."

"You're with the British?"

"Hardly likely." Pullman frowned disapproval. When he opened his mouth again, I noticed his false teeth were rimmed with gold.

I said, "There's only one other service I know of that would be even remotely interested in Jamaica."

"Precisely, comrade," went Pullman. "Only we were trained by them, but we do no actual work for our KGB friends. I work for our Cuban friends."

"You're putting me on again."

"You could also be of some help to *our* Revolution," Pullman said, "if you were truly a friendly person. . . ."

"What are you setting me up to do *now*?"

Pullman drained his cup of coffee.

"The trial is a virtual necessity. Machismo, being the national vice, exoneration seems a public relations certainty."

"What exactly does that mean?" I demanded.

"You must go on trial for your temporary act of insanity. Your Miss Dyllis will also be subpoenaed but on advice of counsel she will not agree to appear. We fix up things anyway, with both the judge and the jury, and, as I say, there is no chance in the world you will be convicted, or, if convicted . . ."

"IF?"

". . . of anything more than a pardon, or a suspended sentence, banishment from the island for life. I assure you of that, Robert. . . . But it is better that the trial never be completed. You will go on trial, a case will be made, and before a deliberation can be brought in, certain elements in the population who are friendly to our revolutionary aims will appear in the courtroom armed and you will be liberated. They will have you taken to Havana. There you will make a statement to the socialist press about your own true motives in executing Seixas. Certain verifications will be provided you. You will be decorated by Fidel, and made an honored citizen of the Cuban socialist state."

"I want to go home," I said: "I don't want to become a citizen of Cuba."

Pullman frowned. "You call yourself a socialist?"

"An American socialist, not a Cuban."

Pullman said, "There is only one socialism in that respect."

He said, "I never thought of you as a hypocrite, Robert."

"We have to get used to these things," I explained. "Just the way I feel about you and murder."

"You don't know what you're saying," Pullman said. "You're just feeling confused. Give you awhile and you'll feel differently, I know that, mon."

"I want to go back home to New York City," I said, "a free man."

"Cuba's the best we can do," he explained. "You got involved and now you *are* involved. Nobody twisted your arm to the breaking point. You had that tendency. Sure we set you up but you let us risk your life. It was your decision. That's the way it happened, Professor, and there is no point in arguing.

"Besides," he added, "I could really use some company down there."

22

Pullman had gone to the sideboard at the other end of the room. He puttered with pots, creamers, and sugarers, and took a long while stirring, humming to himself a little, determined to seem in control.

I thought to myself, look what he's done to my life. . . . Yet I had come to like Pullman. I trusted him, more than myself. He'd reminded me how to kill in cold blood and get away with it. Given me back my youth. When he said he liked me I believed him. He was my only friend in Jamaica at the moment, and he knew it. I could use his company, too.

He was returning with another cup of steaming brew for himself when he said, "My true name is Padillo; I yav the rank of Colonel, and you must not be fooled by my jolliness because I yav a lot of deaths. . . ." At that moment the lights went out.

"Quick Professor," Pullman said, "under your bed."

The rattle of his cup and saucer seemed louder than any Gatling gun. I obeyed orders.

Some window glass in the room shattered. Shotguns were going off, like gasoline drums rattled against concrete; we could hear pellets spray the walls.

In the darkness Pullman had pushed his stout body next to mine, as if to protect me. We couldn't quite fit under the same bed, but we lay behind it as the curtains took the breeze with a swooshing and bellied out into the night.

Then there was another burst of firing, from a machine gun. Pullman said, "That must be our people."

"What's happening?" I asked. "Do you know?"

"Stay down," Pullman said, and then we heard a lot of scrambled Donald Duck noises like a tape makes when it is run over the playing heads backwards. A reggae band commenced to play; the loud voices were chanting some Jamaican names:

> "Mr. Seixas go bang bang
> Professor Harmon go bang bang
> Truth be told de man's extinct
> Dat Mr. Manley's gotten kinked . . . ."

Another volley that went off this time smashed the chandelier above my bed, and glass began to drop down like ice off a roof during a winter thaw.

Again there was an answering burst of machine-gun fire.

Pullman said, "Steady, Professor . . . ."

In the darkness a voice was addressing us: "Mr. Pullman, sir, you should give us de Professor Harmon, please. . . ."

"YOU KNOW WHAT I SHALL BE GIVING YOU," he bellowed back.

Another volley shattered the glass remaining in the windows, and then there was more machine-gun fire, then silence, total silence, and a darkness such as I have never known at any other time in my life. Like millions of insects in a cloud.

Pullman said, after a while, "They'll be going now. It was just to put the fear in you."

"Are you sure?"

"They'll try Macomba next," Pullman said, "black magic,

you know. But they won't ever kill. Don't want to die themselves. So they stay back and threaten, you know. . . ."

"Why?"

"Why not?" he grinned. "It is for the others more than you. So they will think there is really big trouble."

The lights went on again.

Barklay knocked on our door: "Everybody alright in there?"

"We're fine," Pullman said. "Get us a sweeper."

"Be a little while," Barklay said. "There were five of them, all darkies. We chased them to the high road.

"They got one of our boys," Barklay said then. "He's right outside your door. I'll have the guts dragged off."

"Do," said Pullman. "Pity that . . . I didn't think they'd want to kill too. . . . But you can really never tell."

I was feeling so sick to my stomach I thought I could actually smell the man's guts outside our bullet-riddled door.

Then we heard a thumpity-thump as they dragged the body off and when Pullman opened the door I saw only a couple of dark wet spots on the carpet runner.

Not much to remind you of a life. Whoever had been guarding us had stood in the wrong place, I supposed, when the lights went out.

"He must have been one of your men," I said.

"Poor little lummox," Pullman said: "Obeah men come cheap as dust down here. *Patria Libre*. . . ."

"*O morir,*" I added.

"That too," he went. "Death!"

He shut the door and helped me up off the floor, and I was leaning against his all-too-ample body as we surveyed all the open wounds in the windows, and the shreds of glass on the bed and on the rugs, sparkling in the sudden glare from the light overhead.

"I'll have to find you another room," Pullman said, "and we can have more guards posted."

He seemed a trifle shaken himself as he leaned me against a bureau and went out into the hall to make these arrangements.

23

"WHAT WILL I DO in Cuba for the rest of my life?"

It was maybe half an hour later, I was tucked back into a fresh bed, in a freshly made-up room, which looked like a nursery, or child's room; the chairs and counterpane were covered in chintz, and there were illustrations from Mother Goose on all the walls.

Pullman sat at the foot of my bed. He seemed very concerned about my comforts.

"I don't think I want to spend the rest of my life in Cuba," I told him, again, "even with you, as company."

"Shouldn't be that long," he said. "We're expecting a normalization of relations with the U.S. by and by, but Cuba will remain an anomalous socialist state."

"And then I can go back?"

"Before you kick off? *Certainly,*" Pullman grinned. "In the meantime you will be a revolutionary hero. . . ."

"With that and a dime," I said: "Would I be permitted to teach?"

"You'll have to be suitably reeducated in our cane fields," Pullman explained, "or on one of our other state farms. But afterwards, perhaps, you could be some sort of student advisor. You see, Professor, we don't normally stress bourgeois politics in our curriculum."

"Then what would I do to keep busy?"

"You could write, which you claim to like doing, or you could be some sort of agent like me," Pullman said, "ensnaring others, for a very good cause. You've rather a knack for that, I've noticed. So we'll be friends. I like you. I told you that, and I meant it, too. I don't intend to stay on this damn stinking island forever playing policeman for *these*...."

He stopped himself as if astonished by the vehemence of his dislike for all things Jamaican.

After a little while, I said, "You'd be part of the takeover here, of course."

"What takeover?"

"When the revolution takes over all of Jamaica," I said. "The socialist transformation..."

Pullman said, "You foolish *mon,* we like tings just the way they are down here, like them stagnant. Not too much suffering. Not too much hope. Not too many transformations. The more Jamaica stagnates the more Cuba develops, by contrast, and the more the point of our Revolution is affirmed. We can only benefit from such a contrast. But taking over de whole god damn island, that would be giving ourselves an awful headache."

"I didn't realize you were that cynical in Cuba."

"Certain to be," said my new KGB chum, "and it would be such a terrible headache for all of us, to get involved. This island is overpopulated and under-developed. They are going to eat each other alive down here if they are not careful. So we simply want to make sure the old ruling class don't come back in their old ways and that is why Mr. Seixas had to be put out of business. He was fairly competent, you know. Now that class invests its money elsewhere and these incompetent Social Democrats run the show; and everything is just the way we like them to be, stagnant; because they have paralyzed each other, you know."

Pullman got up and pulled his dashiki down across his broad paunch. Strutting about he commenced to sing:

> *"If I were a millionaire I should not be poor.*
> *If they let me grow ganja, who would grow sugar?*
> *Better I dig for aluminium yams*
> *than build cisterns for water, or dams,*
> *so I wish I had a million pounds sterling,*
> *or a yacht full of pussy in Bimini,*
> *apartments on Eastern Parkway . . ."*

He stopped himself, laughed toward the ceiling, and started humming the tune, "Mm mmm mm mm . . ."

"That would be contemporary Jamaica for you," Pullman said. "Social Democracy."

"Did you just make that up?"

"Be a People's Party song," he smirked. "The Mighty Sparrow wrote it, yours very truly, Laughing Jack Thrush. How do you like it?"

"Charming."

Plumly, the servant, brought in a fresh pitcher of hot water and as he fussed with all the cups, Pullman said, "Let me tell you a story. This all happened to me it was some years ago in the sixties."

He sat down on the bed once more and nodded to dismiss the jittery Plumly.

"I was still a student in Georgetown, Guyana, place where I was born. . . . Students are hungry little beasts. I was hungry all the time at University. Never could get enough to eat, you know. So we used to do these different things just to eat. We would go to parties. It was at this party at the American

Embassy to which we were all invited," Pullman said, "and it was mostly for all the good food and drink I was there. Stuffing my face, just like the others. . . . So there was this one man there, one of your own people," he added, "and his name was Welch, though I don't think I knew that at the time. He was introduced to me as the third secretary, or something, but I noticed the way all your Embassy people kept pretty clear of him, and so did I, at first, preferring just to stuff my face. He comes up to me finally. He was quite bold, really forward, considering I was a 'native'; and how could he know who I really was? It was in the papers just then about your CIA infiltrating all the student movements and he asked what I thought about that. I said I thought it was damn shitty. He tried to convince me it was all quite harmless and that nobody had really been corrupted, ordered about, or persuaded to lie. I considered the matter only a lively cocktail party debate but this man, whom I have since learned to call Welch, he invited me to his home after the party. There he proceeded to pump me all about Mr. Cheddi Jagan and his wife Janet, and about all the functionaries I knew in the Guyanese PPP. . . .

"He even took me out to dinner later," Pullman explained, "and then he went into a long elaborate explanation of his forthcoming marriage with a Latino woman. He had obtained, he said, some sort of special State Department dispensation to do so. I don't know why I was supposed to care. The man was confessing something," Pullman said. "He seemed frightened. He was pumping me, yes, but he was also testing the water. I think he knew he was doomed, you see. It turned out he had much more information on me than I had on him, and he knew how poor I was, and who my friends were, what my politics *really* were. He was making me some sort of offer, don't you know? To come over to his side . . ."

Pullman stared at me as if he was reenacting the primal

espionage drama, and I was being stupid, or callous. Worse than that; opaque.

He said, "If I did not take his bait, it was because my own cover was too important. It had to be sustained against all illusions and misinterpretations. We were serious people in those days," Pullman added, "and I thought no more of that strange debriefing session with Welch until some years later when, like him, I had seen much nasty tradecraft.

"It was only a few years ago," he went on, "when it all made sense. I was in London, and I wanted to know what was happening in the world, and I bought a copy of your American magazine, Newsweek, and there was the face of this Welch person again. He'd been murdered in Athens, by *'terrorists,'* or perhaps by your side, because he was a *'double,'* and I was taken back to that Georgetown cocktail party again and his pumping me about the Jagans, and the invitation to have that nightcap, don't you know?

"It made sense to me then, what he was about, and I was just sorry for him. He was just this earnest, slightly stupid, misled American civil servant, in over his head, Robert. I didn't like him. If I hadn't been so hungry I would not have sat a minute with him. But he had bought me a meal when I was hungry. I was sorry, you know, he'd been killed."

He touched my arm again, and I felt his closeness, a warmth. "It is as true of our side as it is of the other. We do work for ingrates, and we sometimes perish. I am most often terribly frightened," Pullman confessed. "All my life I have tried very hard to avoid that."

I said, "I wish I knew what to make of your story."

"Did you think I was some kind of fanatic?" Pullman's gaze was thick with tears. "Save yourself, Robert. I like you, but I'm feeling used up, and tired. . . ."

His eyes were running. He did look exhausted. If only I could console him somehow...."

Pullman yawned and stretched. "When Welch died I knew someday I would also die. You know, it was my first intimation of mortality. Very first I had."

"Sorry."

"It's not your fault," Pullman said. He yawned again. "Mind if I finish off the job you started with Marina? I'm really rather sleepy, but I have such a difficult time falling asleep at night alone."

"Be my guest, " I told him, "if there is such an expression."

"We say simply, 'Good of you old man,' " went Pullman. He got himself up again. "Here's to the Revolution, the People of Jamaica...."

He downed another cup of coffee, as if it were a tonic.

"I was such a greedy young gnat," Pullman said. "I was just hungry all the time. You know . . . a blood-sucker.

"I suppose I was just like Welch," he said, "but at the time I did not know that, and I had contempt for this Welch. I thought we thought differently."

"And now?"

"You must go to Georgetown sometime," Pullman said, "and see the people Welch thought he could keep from Communism. They are living inside garbage cans.

"At least we don't do that anymore in Cuba," Pullman said.

"I still don't want to go," I told him.

"I'm tired," Pullman said. "We'll talk about it again tomorrow."

"How do I know you won't have me killed tonight?"

Pullman looked very hard at me from the doorway. "You don't. But have you any other choices? You know, old fellow," he added, "the trouble with knowing things you shouldn't know is you have to live with them, and so do I. By all rights, you should be dead because you know too much, and you would be dead, if the world were entirely just and fair, and I was just another honest civil servant, but I told you I like you, and I do, *I like you*," Pullman gasped, "so you're not, and Welch is, because he wasn't liked, and let's leave it at that."

"But why do you like me?" I asked.

Pullman said, "You just have a little guts, you know, and you did something for me and my friends and we are grateful to you for that. Now go to sleep, old boy, and we'll talk in the morning. There'll be a man stationed nearby if you get too scared, and if you're horny," Pullman said, "there's . . ."

"Forget it," I told him.

"Just as you like."

24

I DREAMED I WAS a Revolutionary Hero of the Cuban People. This pretty much amounted to laying about at a café table such as they have next to the sidewalk at Victor's Cuban Café on New York's Upper West Side.

A number of beautiful young women dressed in combat fatigues, AK47 rifles on their shoulders, were always stopping by to chat with me.

Then Pullman came along and all my admirers disappeared.

He had a new assignment for me. I was to go on up to Kingston again and murder Marina by stuffing something very hard into her mouth so that she choked. . . .

Morning announced itself when a male servant knocked three times on my door, and presented me with coffee and sweet milk. "Professor Harmon is expected on the verandah for Sunday breakfast in twenty-five minutes."

We were both shaken considerably by the large doll dangling from a hangman's knot in my window. Dressed in my old shorts, it had a professorial pasteboard clapped against its crown, and its hands and feet had been lopped off with a machete so that brown straw poked through all around like dried blood.

"Dat *poupée* be for you?" the servant asked.

"Mr. Pullman warned me," I said, "they would try to scare me. It's really nothing."

But the thought that somebody had been in my room, or outside my window, had me trembling. I loosed the knot so that the doll fell to the garden below, and told the servant he was to get one of Mr. Barklay's men to find the thing down there, but as I showered and dressed I felt a little restored. The morning air was fresh, coffee delicious, and all seemed calm about the house. Some guards had been posted outside the various rooms, and when I hobbled down the stairs I was directed toward the verandah by another black fellow in whites.

Along one of the many corridors I passed two servants gossiping. The first said, "Bascomb bought it last night."

"*Fe* sure," said a comely young woman, making up a bed: "It happens sometimes."

"Like bossman Seixas?"

"Bit different dat," the man pointed out: "He died a rascal's death, dat one. . . ."

They laughed together and then I heard a thrashing of clothes, a face being slapped.

"Got no time for dat today, Mr. Crystal. *You hear?*"

On the verandah every variety of tropical fruit was spread out on great platters at a buffet with urns of coffee and tea. The guests sat in high cane-backed easy chairs around a rather long table. They all carried side arms.

Looking hearty and robust, Pullman clung to Marina's hand, just like a suitor. There was Barklay, very much the master of his own house, at the head of the table, and a young English fellow, with blonde hair and freckles, who looked as if he'd just come down from university somewhere. He wore the same blazer as Barklay had worn last evening, perhaps the very same one.

A pair of black policemen were posted outside the verandah with rifles.

As I stepped onto the porch everybody halloed me, cheerily enough, and when I went over toward the buffet Mrs. Barklay appeared.

She wore khaki safari clothes, a skirt and jacket, and she carried a pistol in a black leather holster that might have been designed by Halston or Gucci. A very good looking blonde, blue-eyed, thoroughly tanned and trim American late model, custom-tailored Valkyrie was my first impression of Binny Barklay, except that this million dollar beauty also seemed to wish to be friendly. "I don't believe we've ever met. . . . Who are you?"

"I'm Robert Harmon."

"So you're the man in our nursery. The man who called. O but of course," said Mrs. Barklay, with considerable warmth, "you stayed over last night because you were injured and I'm afraid they gave you a very rough time. I'm *so* sorry."

From the glances she was getting from Pullman and Barklay she seemed to be saying more than was necessary.

Mrs. Barklay's face reddened, as if she couldn't help herself; was glad for the company.

She poured coffee for herself and me, and then recommended a slice of the papaya, and a handful of the genips, which had both been picked fresh that morning, she explained.

"What are genips?"

"The little green things which look like testicles all in a bunch . . . so shrivelly . . . and delicious," went Binny Barklay. "I'm surprised you've never tried them, Mr. Harmon. They can make your lips pucker. Here, I'll show you."

She plucked a genip off a stem and peeled away its green outer skin with her thumb and forefinger, revealing this globule of estrous pink flesh, which she brought up to her mouth and worked against her teeth, without swallowing: "Simply heaven," she said, "but watch out for pits. Try one?"

"I'll take some for later."

I grabbed off a handful.

"Remember what I said about pits," went Binny Barklay, "and speaking of pits, what do you think of my husband's new boyfriend?"

Her voice wasn't extra loud, but it was meant to be overheard.

"Cute and kissy," I said.

"I like you, Professor," Binny said, "let's have breakfast together."

I joined her at the place she had reserved for me next to her at the long table.

25

"Somebody left a voodoo doll in my room," I said to Pullman right off.

He looked up from his feeding. "See, what did I tell you, right on time? It don't mean a ting *if it ain't got that swing.*" He grinned at me: "How's it hanging?"

"On a noose."

"Don't mean a ting," Pullman said. "People want you off the island. That's all."

"If you ask me it's that Almondero fellow," said Barklay. "I suppose he thinks a bit of revenge is in order."

"Nonsense," said Pullman. "I know Carlos Almondero and this isn't his sort of stunt. A knife in the back in a dark alley would be more like it."

I shuddered.

Noticing me, Pullman said, "You needn't let your imagination run wild. With Seixas out of the picture Carlos has no bite. He's a scared rabbit. Besides, I've plenty of men around the place to protect you, and tomorrow first thing you'll be going up to Kingston."

"If I get there."

"You'll get there," Pullman said.

Everybody seemed to agree with him, and that was about all that got said about that.

We took to breakfasting, but none of us, except for the boy, seemed very eager or civilized conversationalists. Marina occupied herself by stuffing Pullman, who was reclining now against her bosoms, with slices of papaya, star apple, and red banana; after his outburst, he became withdrawn, with a big contented grin upon his face, and I noticed that she now called him Randy.

Mr. and Mrs. Barklay, I am sorry to report, weren't doing so well; they weren't even talking to each other at all, so it was the youngest of the guests, Ferdy, who held the floor.

Seems he was most interested in the Maroon legends. Ferdy claimed to be compiling a book of translations he called *The Fatted White Calf,* and also a dictionary of Maroon folklore through the University of the West Indies at Mona's exchange program with Cambridge. It was to provide him with a graduate degree.

"I'm just a degree collector," Ferdy explained, for my benefit, I presumed. "Some people catch butterflies. I collect degrees, from all the Commonwealth Universities."

"Do you plan to teach someday?"

"Not hardly likely," he explained.

Ferdy, it turned out, was South African, from Bloemfontein. He spoke a very queer patois. Once he dropped a familiar word, *mispocha,* to explain the kinship systems of the early slaves.

Such a curious *spritzing* way of chattering. He prattled, this Ferdy did, non-stop, about circumcision rites, and the like.

"The *kaffirs,*" he said with a permissive affection for his own racial slanders, "have some rather peculiar ceremonies involving a centipede, and certain other queer little beasties."

"REALLY," went Barklay, so totally false *blasé* for the occasion.

Nobody else seemed to want to contribute to their conversation.

Ferdy said, "A matter of bruder to brooder to brother. . . ."

"Why not sister to sister?" put in Binny Barklay.

"Terribly macho society," Ferdy explained. "They glorify the penis, as object, as generational totem, and I'm told even their weapons were shaped to resemble the male glans penis. Quite a *sticklach* that," Ferdy went on, batting his cold blue eyes my way. "Ask Professor Harmon."

He went, "Do you *dig* folklore, Professor?"

"Just a *shmeck*," I told him.

"REALLY," went Barklay for the second time.

Ferdy said, "Male semen was sometimes mixed into a paste pounded out of casava."

"Gross!" went Binny.

"It was a sort of *polenta*," I explained. "Honey from the hive."

"HOW WONDERFUL. HOW REALLY INTERESTING," said Barklay.

Marina looked pretty groggy, as if she couldn't follow a word, and Pullman was dozing.

Ferdy said, "There are numerous rhymes about the male organ, and nonce words, to be sure, and there is such a richness to the entire Jamaican tongue."

Binny nudged me and whispered, "He should know."

I hoped she wasn't being overheard.

" . . . *Ah put me han 'pon me kimbo, Ah meck a sudden movement,"* went Ferdy, and then he added, *"Kimbo* is, of course, the native word for hip, and it most probably comes willy-nilly from *akimbo,* joined at the hip, so that one is coming apart, as it were, if one is *akimbo*. You follow? An awful lot of the *kaffir* language reasons by opposites," said Ferdy, "a bit like your black American slang. Head-biting, nail inclusion, and subincision were called *Chamba,* or *Chamma-Chamma.* You have the expression heeby-jeebies, for example. Now it's one of those metaphorical sound representations of the jitters, but it also contains slang words for Hebrew and jitters, as if to suggest that when the Hebrew landlord came around in Harlem (The *Hebe,* or *Heeby* as it were) at the time of the month the rent was due he gave you the *jeebies* . . . meaning that you were unable to just *'creolize'* or relax."

Ferdy was getting himself in more and more trouble with his hostess. Binny nudged me again, and inquired if I was *"kimbo,* excuse me Professor, *hip?"*

"Not really," I explained, "I'm mostly just lost in all that verbiage willy-nilly."

"But don't you feel like coming apart?" Her laughter was ribald. She had pursed her lips very prettily, only to spill some of her coffee by laughing so that one of the servants had to refill her cup immediately.

"Excuse me," she told the fellow. Then, "Sorry to make you do that."

It was the human thing to say.

I felt warmly toward Binny Barklay.

Ferdy said, "The odd thing is about words like *picky-picky* and *licky-licky* in that they both mean greedy."

"Willy-nilly," I added. *"Lickety-split."*

Very flushed in the face, Binny Barklay nudged me again and inquired if I would care to tour her husband's breadfruit plantation.

"With Carlos and his friends out there?" I was rather dubious.

Pullman woke himself from his doze. "Nothing to worry 'bout. Not a bit. My boys are everywhere, and the lady is armed."

"But you mustn't keep him out too long *dear*," said Barklay, grinning at us wickedly: "He's still recuperating."

"Don't you worry, *dear*," Binny replied, all ice.

"And you must be very, very careful with your side arm," went Barklay, again.

"Not to mention his *short arm*," Pullman joked.

My face felt the color of a red banana.

Under the circumstances, how could I refuse such an invitation?

26

A LAND ROVER was parked outside. Binny took the driver's seat. We went down the long driveway lined with conch shells and broken stones and under a winding palm alley, with the sea to our left, and up a small hillside above the surf, and down another.

There were two shotguns mounted in the brackets of the roof; I wasn't feeling scared any more.

Mostly Binny chattered. "You'll really die when you see my husband's breadfruits, Robert. They'll *zonk* you. I know they will."

We passed a small cultivation of yams, and another of cocoa bushes, like St. John's Breads ripening from red to brownish-blackish-green, and we stopped and smelled their pungent earthy richness, and then we came to trees bearing allspice and kola nuts. Laborers, with machetes, were lashed to their trunks pruning at the branches, like frantic monkeys.

Binny said, "My husband employs hundreds of men. Sometimes I feel like Fanny Burney on her Georgia plantation in the old days before slavery was abolished. It's extraordinary to have so many lives at your feet. They're like the dust," Binny said. "Like insects."

She seemed remorseful. We turned behind a small copse

into thickish jungle trail, and, on the other side, where some boulders jutted, were broad green fields in cultivation, but not with breadfruit. Even I could recognize the triangulating broad leaves and fat stems of a ganja cultivation.

Barklay was administering acre upon acre of first-grade smoke. I watched his stoop laborers, like processions of beetles, in leather aprons, go slowly down the aisles between the plants combing off the flowers for their resinous hashish. The air as spicy as a good spliff.

The plants grew shoulder higm, and as far as my eyes could see, was a veritable ocean of herb.

"I told you *our breadfruits* would blow your mind," went Binny.

It had been quite five years since I'd heard that ugly locution, and I winced a little.

Binny was smirking. "Perhaps I should have depicted these as the fruit which produces our bread."

"Delighted," I said. "Marvellous."

Binny asked, "Have you yet tasted some of the crop?"

"It was believed," I explained, "I was in no condition."

"Probably so, Bob.

". . . You don't mind if I call you Bob, do you?" asked Binny. She took my hand, and made a tickle at my palm so that I felt a little hot worm crawl suddenly up my spine.

Said, "Call me anything you like . . . except Rob. . . ."

Binny said, "It's a heavy trip, our ganja. Not just giggle grass. About the best I ever had, aside from those old color and light shows they used to bring up from Acapulco, but heavy you know, like the dead brought back to life."

An overseer passed us on horseback and Binny waved at the fellow as if she knew him.

He descended the promontory and down into the fields,

going slowly through the rows, lashing the ground with a bullwhip where his workers moved ever more slowly, from plant to plant.

Binny said, "It's really quite good stuff. I assure you. . . ."

"I'm not that much of a smoker."

"You're not?" She looked at me even more intently, as if all the more intrigued by my case.

I heard the whip crack once, then twice again.

Binny asked, "What do you do to get high?"

"I fancy beautiful women," I explained.

"O really." She had led me out of the car to a sheloered shady spot behind some boulders. The air was now sweet with the smell of the chaff from the crops below us, though we rdmacndd hidden.

Binny asked, "With, or without their clothing on?"

"You tell me," I said.

She unfastened the top two buttons of her tunic so that her breasts seemed to swell. "Do you really?" I could almost taste her breath in my mouth, she had come so close.

"Really and truly?"

I placed my hand on her soft blonde cowlick of hair, and pushed it gently back.

Her face was very warm.

I could feel her body heat through her clothing.

Her fingers were on my pants. She was opening my fly.

I lifted the hem of her skirt.

Binny wasn't wearing underpants. She must have been a redhead once.

"There's nobody here for me," she said, when I took her against my body. "I've been so lonely for you, Bob. . . ."

Redheads taste quite different from other women. I had quite a meal, and so did she.

Afterwards she stroked me again and again, as if inflating a tire with a bicycle pump.

Binny smiled at me, wanly. "Nothing like the old European custom of second breakfast."

"Nothing like it," I agreed.

A whip crackled.

"My husband and his fucking serfs," Binny said. She seemed to be sitting on my face, but now she slid forward onto my lap again, her skirts falling down across her knees once more. "We'll have to meet regularly for lunch when we get back to town, Bob."

"Do you mean New York?"

"Yes, of course. Where else?" She seemed startled.

"You know, luv," I said, "it appears I may not be getting back so soon. Your hubby and Pullman have plans to send me elsewhere."

"Don't say it. I know," Binny touched my lips with her finger to silence me. "Just trust me that I'm not one of them."

She turned around and took my face in both her hands and kissed me on both cheeks like a little girl kissing daddy before bedtime. We seemed to be feeling very nicely toward each other now, real cozy and warm. Like friends.

Binny sang, *"Mr. Seixas go bang bang!*
Professor Harmon go bang bang!

"I think that's cute," she said, "don't you?"

"It wasn't really like that," I explained. "It was more like entrapment. . . . I had to strangle him in the end."

"I'm sure." She winked at me.

"Seriously," I asked, "do you really think you can help?"

"Trust me, Bob." She touched my lips again.

"In the morning I'm supposed to be going up to Kingston," I explained.

"Trust me," she said, a third time.

She was still across my lap, her skirts flaring on either side of my legs, and without much prompting from me, her eyes closed, her lips parted, she moaned, and seemed to be on the verge of another orgasm.

Afterwards, she said, "O dear, that hasn't happened to me in such a long time. I hope you didn't mind."

"Not at all."

She slid off me onto the ground.

Binny said, "Have you ever read a novel called *The Leopard* by John Hearn?"

"Can't say I have."

"It's very good," Binny said. "But it doesn't really matter; he's a Jamaican. I just wondered if we would have very much to talk about . . . aside from this. . . ."

She made an appealing gesture at me with her hands.

I asked, "Do you think we do?"

"It doesn't matter," she shrugged. "Trust me."

We heard the sound of horses' hooves against rock and then a small procession of black laborers appeared on the hillside accompanied by an Oriental on horseback. As they started down across those blooming fields of herb I saw machetes glinting in the sun.

"That's Big Minh, our overseer," Binny said.

"I used to call this place Tara," she said, "just like in the book, but now I think I'll call it Tararaboomtea, after you, Bob."

"I'm flattered."

"You're very sweet."

"So were you."

"Really and truly?" She leaned close to me again, but I was afraid of being seen and leaned away. I said, "Yes, and nourishing, too. . . ."

Binny grabbed me close to her, and we hugged each other tightly, and pretty soon we were doing it all over again, until my mouth felt very stiff and gluey-tired, and she stopped herself, at a point more or less beyond recall.

"I used to worry that my husband's people would see me,nbut it really doesn't matter. They all know what it's like living with that mean old fag."

Her voice was just so very bitter.

"I'm really very sorry Binny."

"That doesn't matter anymore," she said. "It stopped hurting a long time ago. . . . What do you really think of his latest boyfriend?"

"Ferdy? A callow youth."

"Hardly likely," went Binny, "He's with the Special Branch, South African."

It was now my turn to say, "REALLY!"

"Not so loud," she said. "You shouldn't be that surprised. We only entertain spooks down here. It's a dangerous world, they all say, and a closed world, too, but trust me and nobody will ever get hurt. I know a way. . . .

"Now let's go back before they start to think we've eloped," she said. "I'll visit you in your room, around teatime."

We got up and brushed ourselves off.

I asked Binny if she would mind telling me who she worked for.

"Me?" It was meant as a joke, but she didn't seem to be taking it that way. "I don't always work," Binny said. She pulled me close to her again, and hugged me. "I'm not working right now. Sometimes I even do it for love."

"But when you *are* working," I asked, *"who then?"* It seemed I must be onto something. "I'd really like to know. I'm curious."

She took a step away from me, and the smile on her face seemed to freeze: "I only go with Jewish men I think," Binny said. "You can make of that anything you like."

But she seemed slightly indignant.

"Should I assume you're with the Israeli Secret Service? The Mo . . ."

"Mossad," she corrected me, "and I knew Seixas, *too*, once upon a time."

She looked very unhappy.

I was sorry for her again.

I said, "I didn't mean to ruin your mood."

"It's nothing," she said, "It was a long time ago. . . a lot of silly memories."

She shook her head vigorously, as if to free herself of the past, and by the time we drove off down the road toward the mansion she was laughing again.

27

WE RETURNED TO an empty verandah, shook hands like strangers, said we would visit with each other later.

"Now you should rest," Binny advised. "And please don't worry."

"I know, trust you," I said.

"You get the picture?"

She threw me a kiss and fled inside the big house.

I was limping toward my room, but I saw the library doors were open and went in.

The room was shuttered, green, cool. I turned on the lights overhead and imagined myself transported to some nineteenth century London club room. There were hunting prints on the walls, big leather armchairs, mezzotints of Dickens, Thackeray, and the Lake Poets, and the shelves were heavy with thick volumes of the *Illustrated London News, National Geographic, Country Life,* and *Geo Mundo*.

A volume on the relationship between West Indian creole and the slave dialects of North America caught my attention, and I started to remove it from the shelf when some loose pages fell out onto the polished floor.

It was a color spread from one of the Sunday pictorials on how independence had affected some of the great houses of Jamaica. Posed very near the rock outcropping where Binny and I had just made love, with far fields populated by stoop laborers stretching beyond them, in crisp white safari jackets that matched, stood shoulder to shoulder, hon and deary, Norman and Binny.

A caption underneath read: "Mr. & Mrs. Norman L. Seixas are among the great land holders of Jamaica. Well-to-do, hospitable, concerned about the deplorable living standards of most of the native populations, they frequently give parties and other entertainments for local charities. Asked about social conditions on his island, this handsome twelfth generation Jamaican told our own Gregg Mitchell, 'It's terrible, and shocking, the way some people are required to live out their lives down here. Believe me, if it were in my power to do something about it I certainly would. . .!' "

I studied Binny's face in the photo. She seemed to be suffering from quite severe menstrual cramps.

Poor Binny, poor darling, I thought, two losers in a row.

At least two, I decided. For I seemed to be feeling somewhat jealous again. Could I possibly be falling in love?

I shut off the lights, and closed the louvered doors, and went up to my new room in the nursery again, and undressed, and lay down naked on the big canopied child's bed. The room was bare, uncluttered; no child had occupied it in quite some time. The quilt was all bumpy against my flesh. I drew it down to the foot of the bed and went naked again to open the window shutters.

From my vantage point I could see the other wing of the great house in which I had been originally lodged; some glazers were replacing windows. They leaned against the old house on tall ladders, bracing up those heavy panes of glass with their naked chests and thighs, as if they grasped sheets of ice within their freezing hands.

Even as I watched one of them slipped, and almost lost his

balance. His glass fell and shattered into a million pieces beneath the ladder. He shook his dirty great mop of Rasta curls at the mess below, and descended slowly to find himself another piece of glass.

The man was bleeding profusely. Both his hands were cut, as if with stigmata. On the ground a fellow worker found some old rags, and bound each of his hands and then he ascended again with fresh glass, all very nonchalant, if you please. Or so I thought. Those rags were turning bright with blood very quickly.

I could not let myself watch any longer. Much too painful to consider his pain, and the early afternoon heat, so heavy, and moist, terrific. Looking away, I felt I could really use a siesta.

I had so much on my mind; I couldn't permit myself to think of others. Not even Binny . . .

I had broken out in a mesh of sweat all down along my body some ten minutes later when Barklay tapped on the door and, without waiting for a by-your-leave, entered the room.

"Sorry . . . didn't think you'd be resting."

Frowzeled, frowning, he made no effort to withdraw.

He had chewed away a piece of mustache directly under his nose, or else nicked himself shaving; the effect was somewhat comical, as if he had developed facial mange.

"I was just about to doze off."

"Probably a good idea," Barklay said. "You have a strenuous day ahead of you tomorrow."

He gave a cross glance down at his immaculate white brogues. "Mind if we talk?"

Were we going to have some sort of man-to-man? I wondered just how much Mr. Barklay could permit himself to know and say?

"It won't take me very long," he was saying. "There are just one or two things."

"You talk. I'll listen," I said. "What's on your mind?"
I sat up on my elbows.
Barklay's face seemed to explode obscenely. "Are you . . . er fucking my wife?"
Annoyed, I said, "I can tell you most honestly, no."
"You swear you're not *making* it?"
"Don't push me, Mister."
He turned very grim, and pale, for one so normally red-faced, and grumbled, "I see," as if he understood me only too well.
"Is that all?" I asked, feeling angry. Let him suffer with whatever knowledge he thinks he has, I thought.
Barklay tried to regain his composure by pulling with his lower lip at that mustache again.
"Don't be so cross with me old man," he said, "she's a bit of a nympho, you know . . . that's what all the doctors say."
"Nymphos," I said, "Mr. Barklay, are mythical beasts, like griffins and unicorns. Your wife seems to me to be a normally sexed adult woman, and I find your remarks offensive."
"You're probably right, you know," he said. "But we're friends, Binny and me, in certain ways. You know . . . I'd hate to lose her."
"You won't," I said. "Just be good to her."
"I'm afraid that's rather beyond me," Barklay said. He paced the room. "Can't blame a man for trying to protect his own . . . ."
"Don't put me on," I said.
Barklay asked, "Has she told you about Margaret Trudeau, and about Seixas?"
"Her former husband?"
"She told you all that," he said, glumly, and swallowed hard. "Well, sir, I . . . "
"Will that be all?"

Barklay swallowed hard again: "I believe I've tried to be a good host. I don't like violence. I never could stand violence. The shooting wasn't my fault."

"Forget it."

"You needn't have been so rude." Barklay was pouting at me: "I never could stand rudeness myself."

"I'm tired. I think I shall have to ask you to leave now."

Barklay said, "I could do the same to you, and then where would you be? I gave you Marina," he said. "The best I had, and I had her nurse you, and I've protected you, as best I could. What else do you want? You're still technically a criminal at large, you know, wanted by the police, for murder."

"I know." His message was that he would think nothing of betraying me to anybody to keep Binny around the house.

Why? Why did he need her so badly? Just loneliness, or love?

"What do you really want to know, Mr. Barklay?"

"Call me Phil," he said. "My friends all do."

"Phil," I tried out the name: "What's it short for?"

Barklay ignored my question to ask one of his own. "Does she . . . er . . . like you? You know . . . ." His face had brightened, reddened. He seemed embarrassed to be any more specific. "Does she, you must know what I mean. . . ."

"Mrs. Barklay likes men," I explained. "You must have known that when you married her."

"It was all Pullman's idea," Barklay said. "Then I got to like having her here. We're only together three months of the year. The rest of the time she's in the States, or on the Continent."

"I see."

"I think she and Pullman were involved once," he said. "Once he called her a real heartbreaker. How else would he know?"

"How indeed!" I was annoyed. Pullman seemed to be everywhere in my life; past, present, and future.

In the thick heat we were silent again, accusatory.

Barklay said, "You mustn't think I'm entirely *hors de combat*. I have my moments."

He pronounced it as if speaking of equine things and I didn't think I wanted to hear about any of his moments.

I said, "I'm sure you have your moments, Phil."

"I'm really not such a bad chap," Barklay said. "I could still be helpful to you."

"Thanks a lot." I nodded at him. My elbows were beginning to ache from propping me up.

"Did she take you in the mouth?" Barklay asked.

I closed my eyes, said nothing.

"I could take you in the mouth, too," Barklay said.

I said, "I believe you really could."

"Sure I could. . . I would, too . . . I've done it for others."

"No thanks."

"I'm good when I'm high," he said. "The ganja does it for me. . . ."

"No thanks. . ."

"You'd really like my ganja," he said.

"If you don't get out of here," I said, "I shall be forced to commit more violence."

"Don't be so rude," Barklay said. "I was being nice . . . and you're always so rude."

Our voices seemed suddenly quite loud.

Barklay went, "O the night was pretty hazy when the piccadilly daisy. . . ."

I said, "I'm not interested. Is that plain? Do you follow me? NOT INTERESTED."

I spelled out both words.

Barklay nodded, as if I had suitably squelched him.

"This thing with Ferdy and me," he said, "it's just a thing. He's just a boy. . . ."

"I suppose you could say that," I said.

"Say what?"

"About Ferdy . . ."

"He's just a boy," Barklay announced a second time: "A mere lad."

"Sorry, I don't really care."

"What *do* you care?" Barklay asked. "You're just a little pipsqueak you know. . . and a *womanizer,* that's what you are, Lothario."

"Friends . . . *gentlemen,* please . . . no spats . . . ."

Pullman had entered the room just behind Barklay and stood with his hands on his fat hips: "Looks like I've arrived just in de nick of time."

He stared at Barklay, and then at me. "What are you doing? What have we here? Answer, please."

I was still trying to ponder Barklay's most improbable insult, and so my answer was a trifle indiscreet. "Mr. Barklay was just offering me his services."

"He's not your type," Pullman scolded, and to Barklay: "That's not his *thing.* Didn't you know that?"

"Stop bullying me," Barklay said. "You cut that out."

"Sit down, please," Pullman said, "and let's all have a meeting of minds."

28

I THINK THE reader should know at this point that I have never considered myself even the least little bit homosexual, but I am not anti-. I believe myself to be a tolerant person. Truth is, that mandatory experience of adolescent abandon with another male had somehow evaded me, perhaps because I once came upon my own brother in such a compromising way with, of all people, father.

It was at our bungalow in the Vineyard the summer of the war in Spain; I couldn't have been more than nine or ten. Seeing them together like that evinced such intense feelings of disgust in me that I was nearly catatonic for the rest of the vacation. I think I was probably also a little jealous; father had always seemed to care more for Hal than me. Right then and there I demanded to be sent up to boarding school and I never spent much time with my family after that. But my disgust, and intense loathing for this pair, lingered, and was foremost to my feelings. I felt so very vulnerable, so naked, don't you know, even though I was fully clothed watching them.

I felt, similarly, laid out, naked, in the midafternoon heat, for Barklay and Pullman, and, in fact, I was. Felt as if I might just find myself aroused, in spite of myself, to change the subject, or perhaps save my own skin.

They had taken chairs on either side of the bed, as if they

were sitting up with a corpse. Barklay, I could not fail to observe, seemed to be looking for life signs on only one part of my body.

When I pulled the thin summer sheet over myself Pullman asked if I was feeling cold.

"Are we playing twenty questions?"

Pullman said, "Barklay over there makes a play for all the fellows, though he's not really *that* sexual, are you Barklay? You're rather a bit asexual, I would say, aren't you Barklay, rather asexual, wouldn't you put it that way?"

"Quite true. Very definitely," he said, "I'm rather diffident you know."

"I would say queer, meaning asexual," went Pullman, "wouldn't you?"

"*A*sexual," Barklay squinted, and swallowed hard: "But def. Quite true, I'm afraid."

"No real interest in the act? *Just a tease?*" Pullman insisted.

"I suppose you could put it that way." Barklay stopped himself. He must have been remembering Pullman and Binny together, all sorts of things like that. He said, "You keep on bullying me. I wish you wouldn't."

"Listen to her," went Pullman, "regular Irish teapot."

"May I ask the purpose of this meeting?" I demanded.

Pullman seemed to be melting asexually all around his chair, but now he got himself together again, in a solid massing of sinew and flesh. "To brief you on what tomorrow holds in store for you," he declared, "and also to offer you our good counsel and support, it is perhaps necessary that we review what has transpired so far between the various parties, namely you, and me, and poor Mr. Barklay here who is feeling rather aggrieved, I should think."

"More bull?" I was feeling groggy from all the rhetoric.

Barklay said, "Get to the point, Pullman."

"The point is Rob Harmon really can't believe I admire him for what he was able to do to Mr. Seixas." Pullman grinned at Barklay, like a prompter. "Can you fancy that? Why not tell him, Barklay?"

"Mr. Pullman admires you," The Irishman declared, flatly, "and for what you did to Norman Seixas."

"Thanks very much." I felt in the middle of some farce about manners.

"Truth is," Barklay said, "Mr. Pullman is a bit of a hero worshipper."

"Nice and easy," Pullman put in. "Take it easy Barklay, you can do it."

"Is there anything else I have to add?" Barklay shrugged.

Pullman said, "*He* really doesn't like women. *He* doesn't even like men very much. Asexual is what you'd have to call that, I suppose."

"I suppose so," I said.

"Don't mess around with Barklay's tart," Pullman said. "She's a nice tart but she's only a tart. Say bye-bye to her, do you understand?"

"I'm afraid that's none of your business," I told him.

"She's a tart," Pullman said, "a Quim. She's not worthy of you. Let Barklay have all the headaches. They deserve each other."

"You sound bitter," I told him.

Pullman seemed to flinch a little: "I am only thinking of your well-being, Robert."

A contractile vacuole.

He said, "You need to think about yourself, for a little while."

"I quite agree with you about that."

"We'll be leaving at dawn," Pullman said. "We'll take a thermos and drive straight to my office downtown. Then you shall be arraigned at the assize and your application for bail—which I have already arranged for—accepted. You will be lodged," he went on, "at the expense of our people here in the same suite you occupied previously at the Sheraton. My men will attend you at all times, and you will be allowed visitors, if they have proper ID. Barklay over there," he continued, "will also be available to assist you in various licit ways, and we will meet once a day just to talk, you and I, a few hours at a time . . . and arrange things. Your solicitor is the best on the island. He was Seixas' man. You can ask anybody about Mr. Seixas' man, Solomon, there are none better."

Pullman bit down heavily on those last words with his jaw. "Any questions?"

"I don't think so."

"Anything you want to ask me," Pullman said, "anything at all?"

I thought of Ferdy. Did Pullman know of his connection to the South African Special Branch?

Looking horrified, Barklay went, "Now don't be such an ass," but Pullman was grinning at me, as if I'd made him proud. *"Really,"* he went, as if to imitate Barklay, "well, of course. We're all agents here, you know. Barklay over there free-lances for the Haitians."

"Now really, please," went Barklay. "Enough's quite enough of that, thank you." But he also seemed to be pleading, and whispered, *"He* doesn't need to know."

I asked if there was something else I should know.

Pullman grinned, again, at me, proudly. "He's also done yeoman service for the Royal Canadians, minus Guy Lombardo, of course . . . and as a singleton in the Margaret Trudeau affair." Pullman went over to where Barklay was standing and chucked him across the chin. "Isn't that so, sweetheart? You're a regular slut, aren't you?"

It was more than even Barklay could take. All that goading, that teasing; he just seemed to break apart. "Get your filthy *wog* hands off me," he said. "Don't touch me with those bloody dinge hands ever again. Do you hear me? *Ever again* . . ."

His jaw was trembling, his mustache drooped. He said, "You and your kind won't be top dogs forever. They'll eat you alive just like they did with all the others, and that's the day I'm waiting for, when scum like you are really brought down again."

He'd said too much. Barklay knew it. He couldn't retract any of it. He seemed to back away from himself, from the angry vituperative effigy he'd cast toward his superior and adversary, though Pullman had remained all the while laconic, calm, almost stolid. You couldn't tell what he was thinking. He simply took the insults and the racial epithets, and that grin never entirely faded from his face. Such was his contempt for Barklay it didn't seem to matter any longer what Barklay said, or did. He was finished. It was that simple. He'd had it.

At last, Pullman breathed in the air of the room, as if it was cooling to him, and said, "Very well but we must let Professor Harmon rest, Phillip."

He put a hand on the small of Barklay's back; it was more like a shove, a nudge, a push, and pointed him out the doorway.

"Such a fine gentleman our Mr. Barklay," he said, from the threshold. *"So refined, Robert."*

He wished to share some of his contempt with me, but though I was in agreement I was also feeling sympathy for Barklay in his plight. There was no denying he'd been goaded.

Pullman said, "I really do admire you, Robert, and I know it may seem hard for you to believe but we really are *all* in the same business. It's a matter of who has the best line on you, or should I say—*key*— and at the moment, Robert, I do. . . . I'm your last best hope. . . . I think I should remind you of that."

"I understand," I said, flatly.

"O Lord," groaned Barklay. "Don't listen to this, please."

Pullman said, "Sorry you couldn't get your piece of arse from the Professor, Barklay. Truly sorry . . ."

And then they both left me again.

29

WHEN BINNY CAME up to my room, I was asleep. In the dark she took off her wrap and joined me in bed. Didn't even try waking me. But once, in turning onto my side, I brushed against her, and she woke up. Naked together we clung.

Binny said, "I missed you. It's a bit early for that, don't you think?"

"I'm glad you're here."

"Just glad?"

"At very least," I said.

Binny said, "I'm afraid my case is a bit worse than that."

"You're going too fast," I told her.

"I think I'm mad in love with you," she said. "Don't you feel anything?"

"Feel?"

"Feel me," she said. "I'm so hot I'm about to explode."

After making love we fell apart again. Then she said, "It doesn't matter what you say. I know I really love you."

"You're very sweet."

"You want to know something?"

"Anything."

"When I saw you on the porch, I knew you were different. Not like the others. I just had to have you," Binny assured me. "I was out of control from the first minute but I tried not to show it. And then we took that ride together and I realized you were very precious to me and I had to help you."

"Can you help?"

"Maybe." We lay in gloom a long, long while. I thought she must be dozing except I heard her again: "Robert, Pullman and I were *never* lovers."

"It doesn't matter," I said.

"It matters to me," she said. "I want you to know that. We were *never* lovers."

She grasped me tightly: "Do you understand?"

"I understand."

"Never," she said, "even when Norman wanted it that way, and there was a time I was so in love with Norman I would have done almost anything for him, *anything*," Binny repeated: "Can you understand that?"

"I understand," I said, but I was feeling rather let down. I wanted to believe Binny, and to trust in her, I needed to, but none of it seemed to be making any sense. Pullman called her a tart. Something must have happened.

I found myself asking if the occasion had ever arisen for her to refuse Pullman.

"There have been times I wished I could kill that man," Binny said: "You wouldn't understand. He drags people down. Look at poor Barklay . . . my husband," she corrected herself, as if calling him so impersonally by his last name might be giving me a wrong impression of their relationship.

We were silent again.

Night bled all the light from the room. As it drowned us in its swampy darkness, I felt my fear emerging once again. I had to get away from this place. Could Binny help?

"I love you," she said. "And I'd do anything for you."

She clung closer to me, though I could not respond.

Binny said, "Tonight around five I'll have a car pull up to the house. They'll all be asleep. The driver is an old friend. We call him Excello. Get in the front seat with him and do whatever he says. I'll be meeting you later."

I needed to know more. "I can't risk it," I told her.

Binny said, "Alright. I'll take you myself, fetch you and off we'll go together. Can you trust me?"

I found her hand and held it.

"Can you?"

"Where would we go?"

"My parents have this little place near the Blue Lagoon," Binny said. "They very rarely come there any more. But I sometimes used to go there to be by myself. Or when I was with a lover," she added.

She waited to hear if I would express disapproval.

". . . It's an easy drive into Port Antonio from there," Binny went on. "I have some money. We can charter a fishing boat and head across to Venezuela, or Providencia, or San Andreas. I know people in all those places," Binny said. "They can arrange for us to get transit further on."

"Further on?"

"The Middle East," Binny said: "Israel."

"And then?"

"We'll stay awhile. Have you never been? It's really quite beautiful in the hills above Jerusalem this time of year."

"I doubt if I would feel at home," I said.

"Why not, Bob? I have pots of money. We'll be happy. You'll see."

"I'm no Zionist," I said.

Binny said, "Consider me Zion. A rose of Sharon, daughter of Jerusalem. A lot better than being stuck in Cuba with old Pullman and his wretched friends. We can travel on the Continent frequently, get a place in France. I'll send for my daughter."

"Your daughter?"

"You're sleeping in her bed," Binny pointed out. "She's six years old. And very cute. You'll like Claudia."

"Claudia?"

"Norman's name for her," she said. "But he never really knew her, poor thing. Just pinned that name on her and left me."

"I doubt if she'll be very fond of her father's murderer," I observed.

"You did her a favor," Binny said. "She's an heiress . . . very, very rich."

"Still I . . ."

"She's with my parents now in New York," Binny said. "She could stay with them awhile longer. It wouldn't have to be right away. Barklay never cared to have children around. I just thought you. . . ."

"What about me?" I demanded.

"You seemed so different," she said. "Nicer. For one thing, you had some humor about you, and . . . I . . . what's the matter, Bob? Am I asking too much. Don't you like kids?"

I tried to imagine myself living with Binny and the child of the man I had murdered, and I was suddenly very miserable again, sunk deep in despair. It was as if I would never be allowed to clamber out of this pit others had dug around my life the last few days.

"It's just that everybody wants to make a deal with me, for me," I told Binny, "and they're all in such a great big hurry. It isn't fair."

"I love you," she said. "This isn't any ordinary deal."

"What about me?" I demanded. "Don't I have needs?"

"First you need to live," Binny said. "Survive. Afterwards we can argue about the details. I promise you I won't be possessive."

"All women are."

"I suppose so," she said. "But I'll try not to be."

"Then what?"

"Maybe we'll make a baby," Binny said. "I'll want another baby before I'm too old. You won't have to worry. I told you that. I have pots of money."

Another deal with my life, and this time it involved making new life. I told Binny I was too old. Thinking about a family was out of the question.

"You're not that ancient," she said. "Nobody ever is...."

"I'm not a very responsible person," I told her. "Why do you think I never married?"

Her laughter was harsh: "I thought perhaps you hadn't ever met anybody."

"Would you like to believe that?" I told her. "Would that help?"

"I suppose not." She was silent again.

Then, "Don't you even care?"

"I care."

"No you don't, you fucking bastard. I'm offering you your life. My life too. Everything I've got. You fucking prick bastard worrying about deals. You bastard," Binny said. "You don't even care."

She pulled the covers away and leaped from the bed.

I couldn't see her in the dark but I could hear her rustling through those cast-off garments on the floor.

"Binny," I said, "I have a right to make choices, don't I?"

"Fucking stiff prick bastard," she said. "I just hope they *off* you."

She ran out of the room.

A few minutes later the light flashed on. She stood in the doorway, in her wrap again. "No I don't . . . really."

My eyes were unused to the glare.

She came no further.

Binny said, "Sorry about that . . . just something left over from Bensonhurst."

"It's alright."

She looked a little downcast. "You broke my heart. . . ."

"You never gave me a chance."

"Don't you care about us at all?" Binny demanded.

"Of course. I just can't sell myself like that."

She started to weep. "I'm sorry for you. Really I am."

"I need time to think. To make up my mind. You wouldn't want me to live with you on false pretences."

"THEY'LL KILL YOU," Binny screamed at me, "THEY'LL KILL YOU AND THAT WON'T BE FALSE PRETENCES."

No two angry women look alike: Binny seemed to turn the color of autumn leaves. Again she fled, without shutting off the lights.

Moments later Pullman appeared.

"I thought I heard screaming? Could it have come from here?"

"I think I heard something too," I said. "But maybe it was just an owl, or the wind. It woke me."

"We *don't* have any owls in Jamaica," Pullman said. *"Doubt* if we ever did."

"Then it was some other bird. . . ."

"O yes, be some other bird." The sly grin he left me with was an acknowledgement of his complicity and reassurances.

30

THE SERVANT WHO normally brought breakfast to Phil Barklay in bed at 6:00 A.M. was greeted by a truly heart-stopping sight when he opened the door to his master's room and almost lost his footing in a rivulet of slippery blood.

On the large brass bed lay a pair of male lovers with their arms about each other; they were both headless.

Barklay and Ferdy had each been neatly decapitated with one clean swipe of a machete and their heads then hung like Jack O'Lanterns in the bedroom window.

There was considerable consternation about the house thereafter. As Pullman explained it to me over coffee at 6:30, it was more than likely the work of Carlos Almondero. "A matter of tit for tat," he explained. "This will probably be the end of it, though," he believed. "Carlos is spent. He'll just fade into the woodwork now. Old Carlos has a healthy respect for his own skin,"Pullman observed.

He was already making arrangements for disposing of the bodies. A mortuary truck was expected; Mrs. Barklay had been notified, but preferred, he said, to stay abed.

With a wink he told me, "Her grief is *truly* very profound."

He told me that despite the unfortunate incident we would

be leaving for Kingston together in fifteen minutes. Did I care to view the ghastly scene of the massacre?

I demurred.

Pullman was not allowing himself to feel very much about what had happened. I tried to emulate his coolness.

He asked if there was anything I needed to do before we left, and I requested that somebody help me change the dressing on my wound.

He went into his room and woke Marina. She came to me with her eyes still half shut from sleep and applied a new gauze pack.

Watching her all the while, as if jealous of her attentions toward me, Pullman said, when she had finished, "That will be all Marina. Get some rest."

She left us alone again.

"Poor old Barklay," he said then, "I'll bet he never knew what hit him. One clean swipe for each of them with that chopper sufficed. The man has good wrists. Must have been a cane cutter once upon a time."

"So you don't think it was Almondero?" I was getting back into my clothing.

"I didn't say that," Pullman said. "What made you think that?"

"Nothing, but you seemed so sure before."

"If you're trying to trick me into confessing, it won't work. I'm the law around here, not you." He seemed very cross with me, and I said nothing more because I had a long trip into Kingston with him ahead of me now, and I had to be very, very careful, if I didn't want to jeopardize my safety.

I said, "The whole thing is so horrible. I just thought. . . ."

"You just thought one too many times," Pullman said. "Get dressed; or I won't be sorry."

But once we were in the back seat of the Land Rover with the two armed constables up front, Pullman was calm, and friendly again. He asked after my comfort, and told me I was to sound off, if I needed to stop at any point.

"It's a pretty drive," he said.

"They all are."

At Spanish town, at a BP station, I asked for permission to stretch.

Permission granted, with constables, in arms, flanking both my sides.

Then we drove on, mostly through cultivations of sugar, until we began to see the signs for Port Royal. Pullman seemed preoccupied with official papers he was carrying in a leather case, but at the point where the road forks off toward the sea he told our driver to stop again, and got out, and stepped down into a ditch, and relieved himself in the direction of its spillway.

He had taken his stance in profile to the road, a giant of a man, with his big dorkus like a flail; the dark fish holding it moved it up and down and around and around through the steamy air in intricate figure 8's. He seemed to be as impressed with his range and velocity as any small schoolboy and when he caught me looking again the same sly silly grin took his face once more, so that I had to glance away fast, because I was speculating on last night's carnage and it occurred o me that Pullman could have "offed" them both; he had the wrists for it, and the strength, and a motive. Another perfect cover-up. . . .

And when he came back into the car we did not move right off so that I thought now it was going to be my turn in that same ditch with a pistol to the back of my head, among the cattails, and detritus, soaking in Pullman's urine.

He said, "I haven't done that since I was a boy."

"Piss?"

"Wobble it about like that," Pullman said. "Miss Marina surely puts the joy of life back into a man."

He laughed.

"Not exactly the most picturesque part of Jamaica, is it?" He pointed out the window.

The land beyond the ditch had been graded, and the dust was flying. A red-on-yellow signpost stuck up proclaiming that here the American firm of J.I. Kislak, Inc., "The Live Wire Agency," would shortly construct a large industrial park. A number in Miami Beach was posted for inquiries. From the weathered look of the sign I gathered there had been few inquiries. And all the rest of the neighborhood seemed equally abandoned, though ungraded.

Pullman said, "These used to be rice and sugar cultivations. But the land is just much too valuable, you know."

I found I had trouble swallowing my saliva, or even producing any.

Pullman was buttoning his trousers, but now he reached for the batch of papers to one side of his lap and selected one dark thermofax sheet on which a paragraph in white had been imprinted, and handed it over to me, as if to pass it beneath my nose.

A sour chemical odor suffused my nostrils as I commenced to read:

> Gonsalves, Rafael, b Havana, Cuba,
> 2/28/36, Nat. U.S., University of
> Chicago 1962, AB, MA Columbia,
> 1964; State Dept. press of GS-14
>   65–67; ECA, Portugal, 1968, USIA,
> Jerusalem 2/69 . . . R

That R wasn't any news to me, as I told Pullman, who said:

"Your State Department stopped printing these biographical registers after 1974. Those R's—Mr. Welch's demise in Athens was responsible for that."

"I seem to recall something to that effect," I said.

"So you are aware your Mr. Gonsalves is a covert op?"

"It really isn't any of my business."

"It doesn't upset you?"

"Sometimes you surprise me Pullman," I said. "You expect me to be even more naive than I really am. It's as if I grew up believing my father was cruel and all you do is keep showing me what my cruel daddy has just done. Well, who ever said I expected otherwise?"

"Is that so?"

"So," I said. "It's so, believe me. *Das hat er!*"

"Very good," said Pullman, and told our driver to move on.

31

As we came to the suburbs of Kingston I glanced out through the rear window of the Land Rover and saw Binny, two cars behind us, her hair catching the wind, in an open blue sports car.

She wore a white aviator's scarf of considerable length around her neck, and seemed to be intent solely on keeping up with the traffic.

Pullman noticed I was looking. He said, "Mrs. Barklay is it? She must be really taken with you to be so indiscreet."

"What would she be doing now at Savannah-la-Mar?" I asked.

"Mourn," went Pullman. "That would only be proper."

I said, "She's a good woman. She may need to be with other people."

"She may need more than that," Pullman later said, "and you know it, mon, don't you?"

We came to the buildings that housed the Justice Ministry and some courts and Pullman had his driver park in a vertical space and escort me out across the lot to the infirmary.

A police officer was waiting for us at strict attention. So much had happened to me in the last forty-eight hours that I did not recognize Brigadier Erskine until I heard his voice, like orders barked across a drill field: "Ah Pullman sir, and I believe you have our prisoner. Ready to give himself over?"

"Quite."

The Brigadier next greeted me: "A good morning to you, Professor. Fine day. You look rested!"

"Thanks."

"Will that be all?" Erskine inquired.

"*All*," went Pullman.

He started as if to leave, and I felt so fearful all of a sudden I couldn't just let him. "Come with me."

"Professor . . . ?"

"Please . . . please . . . come with me."

"Just as you like, Rob." He draped an arm across my shoulder.

The three of us entered the Magistrate's office together where I was fingerprinted, and asked to sign an affidavit for bail.

Then I was introduced to Mr. Solomon, my solicitor, who simply told me, "Now don't you fret about another thing." We were led from the anteroom into the main chamber.

The courtroom was virtually empty. Mr. Solomon was small and kidney-bean colored; he wore a white summer suit, and a smart white straw hat.

The judge was vast and black, in his robes; his small oval-shaped head was topped by a large white wig.

I was asked to sit at the counsel table with Erskine and Pullman behind me, and then Solomon went up to the bench, with the Queen's own, a wiry man in an open guayabera shirt, and they conferred some moments, and then returned.

Solomon was smiling at me wryly.

The Magistrate gavelled us to attention.

Application for bail had been granted.

We were all being released, until further notice.

In the anteroom Mr. Solomon bowed at me obsequiously. "I shall come to visit you and we shall talk about your witnesses. It won't matter. Nothing matters anymore," Solomon said. "Be sure of that.

"This above all," Solomon told me, wagging his finger: "is Jamaican justice, and if you ask after that if Jamaican justice is truly just, you must ask somebody other than a Jamaican. You should be the best witness to that, eventually, Professor!"

He smiled, baring little dog teeth, and then he and Erskine departed, to look over their various pieces of evidence.

"This is the shit of modern nationhood," Pullman said to his back. "You could take a cab to your hotel, if you like, Robert," he told me, "though perhaps I ought to drive you just this once, for the sake of our friendship."

In the Land Rover he was grinning: "That wasn't so bad, now was it?"

I had to admit it was not.

When he dropped me off in front of the Sheraton, Pullman said, "Taking off for Negril for a few days with Miss Marina. You behave yourself, Rob, while I am away. Do you hear me lad?"

"I'll miss you," I told him: "I'll worry."

"You'll be closely watched."

"Pullman," I asked, "did you chop Barklay and Ferdy?"

"By all means," he said, grinning again: "And if you don't believe me, mon, ask Miss Marina sometime, because she helped."

Pullman revved his motor at me, loudly.

Until he was somewhat calmer I waited, before asking him about the money.

"What money?"

"You promised me $100,000."

"Jamaica is a very poor country, mon. No way."

"It was a promise, Pullman. . . ."

"You crazy, mon," he told me, before speeding off into the dust so that I was left standing against a hurricane fence, beyond all that hot tarmac.

He's got to be kidding me again, I told myself. Got to be.

32

A COUPLE OF messages were filed in my name at the front desk when I registered.

The handwritten note from Binny came on pale blue stationery in purple ink redolent of orange blossoms: *Darling, lovers always scrap. I've taken the suite just below you. We'll get it together and chat. I know you'll see the thing my way. Even if you don't do it better than anybody I've ever known, like it says in the song, you're pretty darn good . . . and men got no right to expect that sort of shit from women any more. . . .*

Love ya
B
(Widowed)

There was a much longer letter on foolscap, typed, rather imperfectly, in pigeon pecks, by the man who signed it, Carlos Almondero:

> *Dr. Harmon you surprise me, sir. More and more. I should be so very angry at you when I am not. You have to do your work and I have to do my own.*
> *But poor Mr. Seixas, his number was up, and Bark-*

lay you know what I mean, man, he was some big maricon....

You are a very brave man, as you must know by now, and I am not some little **gusano,** *so why not we get together? I could like to help you if I be in your service, and to be your employee, sir.*

You could probably always use a person such as me, in the States, too, for I could speak double languages, Spanish and English, and I must have only what I need for my pockets.

Perhaps, if I pay you a visit, we to talk of situations of mutual advantage to our both selves.

Beyond that you should know I am a first class driver, and mariner, and I have the ability at flying the Piper Cubs. Also, I was trained at Camp Perry which you would call "The Farm," and I am skilled with such various pieces of equipment for self-defend. Plus a black belt in Judo.

I am, too, a skilled communicator, inter-mediate range frequencies.

So I hope you will consider my proposals and did not scoff at me for coming to this point as I am now.

We could be associated, in good ways, and bad, I think.

I will call on you sir, and we will talk. Have not too much fear. The malice I bear you is varnished. **Patria Libre.** ...

Almondero

There was such a formalistic quality to the language of Almondero's communication that it took me a good little while to figure out the little pie-faced man meant *vanished*.

Then I noticed a strip of contact prints he had enclosed inside the envelope.

The same old waltz with different waltzers: Pullman in Binny's mouth, and vice versa. It was as if the conspiracy I'd stumbled into was a daisy chain. But all I kept thinking about was what liars all agents are. You can't trust a single goddamn word any spy tells you. Mr. Cord Meyer Junior as newspaper columnist is probably no more reliable than he was as a professional scoundrel working for the Agency.

Those were the thoughts I had in my room when I considered the fact that six or perhaps seven intelligence services were now bidding for my services (I'd lost count), including Almondero, a war unto himself, and I hadn't yet gotten a straight story from any of them but they'd offered me just about every other inducement to my greed: love, money, fame, fear. I thought if I was really lucky, I could still pick and choose, or not at all; the trouble with liars is they lose track of what's truthful themselves, and then you have to remind them it was all their lie, to begin with. Meantime, I was living in the best hotel in Kingston, at Government expense. Afterwards might come book offers. I was sure they would. I'd always wanted to write a spy book.

I savored such prospects, like a glass of old brandy during a winter rainstorm.

Had I blundered my way into a maelstrom of gold? Pullman and I had money matters to talk about yet. . . .

I thought of the publicity the whole affair must be getting worldwide. Something a little different than writing monographs on the Federalist papers, or revisionist views of the Cold War.

Probably my chairman and dean would object to some aspects of my new public image. They would have to, for the sake of form. Like, we never hire our own graduate students. All for the sake of good form.

I glanced out the window down onto the bright azure surface of the pool. My picture had made all the papers. Today's *Gleaner* might be featuring head shots of Barklay and Ferdy, but I would still be the one people recognized. If I went down to take a swim, I'd be mobbed. Women would offer me their bodies. Patriots might demand my autograph. No wonder Binny was so damned interested.

Still I found I had anger toward her for manipulating my feelings, and toward Pullman, too. He had connived to get me into such a mess.

Despite the fact that I was now feeling fairly confident I would survive my vacation in Jamaica, I craved a sort of revenge, after all.

It wasn't so hard to devise the perfect antidote to all my poisonous hate, and jealous anger. In the night table drawer was some stationery. I wrote out a small advertisement for the *New York Review of Books* which I mailed with a check that would have more than covered the amount due; I later learned this ran under *Personals:*

> *"West Indian gentleman, big and jolly, for a government employee, fond of French and Greek, and good at Russian, with blonde American consort, having similar interests, seek visitors for extended playful vacation their island paradise. Company and pleasure. Send photos ASAP. All expenses paid. Write Pullman-Barklay, Tiddler's Bay, Jamaica, BWI"*

I also asked that the surplus money be used to send copies to me at the same address.

I thought, for sure, they'd read that one in Langley, and probably in Havana, too, and Moscow, not to mention good old Kingston town. So I had blown Pullman's cover, as neatly as a fistful of dandelion fluffs, and now perhaps he would have to scramble.

Delighted with myself, I mailed the letter at the desk and went upstairs to my room again.

I really don't dislike turncoats, but I certainly can't admire them. The *Gleaner*, which I purchased told of Binns, the downstairs servant, who was being held as an "accessory" to the murder of his master, and probably would confess to something or other, eventually.

Somehow the thought of a rich corpse like Seixas being able to afford "accessories" for his murder tickled me no end. I wondered what they would do to poor Binns.

A ringing phone greeted me as I came back through the door of my suite after being in the lobby.

The man at the desk said Mr. Gonsalves, the American Consul, wished to visit with me. He wanted to know if this was a convenient time for such a visit.

I asked that he be sent up, and told the desk to call Room Service and order a bottle of Appleton Gold Label, and the fixings.

Moments later that gaunt seersucker figure appeared in my doorway.

He said, "You'll be happy to know I've been reading all your books while you were out of town.

"Good to have you back in town, Professor Harmon," added as blandly as ever, like a headwaiter inspecting a crepe suzette, but with that distaste for the inside of his mouth which screwed the expression on his long dark pock-marked face a little sour. "Now I see you've come back just in time to face the music."

He grinned at me like half a million dollars.

"I've ordered some refreshments," I said: "Perhaps we can talk."

"*Claro.*"

He took himself over to the most comfortable chair, and

hitched up his trousers to reveal black silk socks with silvery clocking, and a bit of practically smooth hairless calf.

"I suppose you know, sir, your activities down here have made all the stateside papers. It's the biggest intelligence caper we've had since Francis Gary Powers—maybe even before that."

"Sorry if I've caused you any trouble."

"Not a bit," Gonsalves said, "but you understand my people are sensitive. One thing to run agents. Quite another for university professors to work as assassins."

"Is that what people are saying?"

"That's what *some* people are saying." Gonsalves leaned much closer. "Your ex-dolly gave out with an interview."

"Did she now? Really . . ."

"*Really,*" he said. "Professor, you're in trouble."

"You mean you are."

Gonsalves' face was without expression.

". . . If you're really State Department, and not Agency," I asked then, "why bother me?"

His head shook as if it had been bugged by a fly. "You make the most unnecessary distinctions sometimes."

He took out his little pad and paper, and wrote: "I've come with an offer."

"Yes, of course," I said right back at him, "and stop with all the secret writing because it really doesn't matter. Nobody can keep a secret in Jamaica."

"I suppose you're right." He was grinning a little when the drinks arrived and I excused myself to sign for the chit and tip the bellhop.

After I had poured out two strong ones I asked if the Consul would care to stay for lunch.

He said he was in a hurry just now but I ought to try and hear him out.

"Yes, of course." I was thinking Gonsalves wasn't the sort of man to gossip idly.

"I'm sure you've had a lot of other interesting propositions," he said. "My people don't haggle and we don't bargain. In the developing world we're the best and we're not in competition with anybody. . . . We want you back—*with us*."

"So I've heard . . . from others." I was grinning.

Gonsalves said, "We know what your situation is. How desperate you must feel."

"*O*? I'll get by."

"Mr. Pullman is a cold-blooded murderer," Gonsalves said: "Did you know that?"

"He chops mean pork," I said, up toward the ceiling, hoping we were being listened to.

Gonsalves said then, "If you took my word you could leave here in twenty-five minutes by plane."

"Twenty-five minutes?" It seemed like such an odd interval of time.

I said, "Would I have time for a shave? Let's make it a half an hour."

"I'm off on home leave tonight to Puerto Rico," Gonsalves pointed out: "You could walk out of this room in my company and come with me to the Embassy and nobody will dare to bother you. We would leave on a military flight. Nobody would dare to interfere if you were in my custody. And then, after a few days' rest, you'd be allowed home again."

I was so used to all the proposed deals by now that I asked, "And then what would I have to do?"

"*Do?*" Gonsalves had a hole card. "There's nothing you *can* do for us except teach your classes at Columbia, just like you always did. That's about it. Just do your job, as always, and I'll have you wearing mink coats with Astrachan collars. The

Agency can arrange for you to be reinstated, and that will be the end of that."

"Just like that?" I asked.

"Like that just exactly," said Gonsalves. He suddenly looked earnest like cartoon pictures I have seen of Frank Snepp. "Professor Harmon, we need good men like you in our universities training good tough-minded students to think. *The West needs those minds,*" he said. "The Cubans are in Africa. The Russians are about the Horn. The Shah is in the Bahamas. The Saudis are frightened for their oil. Around the Horn it's getting fairly sticky. As an old hand, can you follow me?"

"You mean recruitment?"

"The Agency has gotten perhaps a little bit moribund in the last few years," he told me. "The old guard are all retiring. Pearson's dead and buried. They're all pretty much out of the picture."

"You want me to serve in their place?"

"Professor Harmon," he said, "we happen to have a lot of competition, and I don't only mean from abroad, even in our own country there's NSA, land satellites, you get the picture, software, and brains, are hard to beat."

"How would I be able to contribute?" I inquired, a trifle *faux* naively, because I was having such a very good time just hearing him out.

Gonsalves said, "Nobody has yet replaced person-to-person contact for information, but we need people who put ethical considerations first. Patriots. Good citizens . . . tough minds. . . ."

"Like I was, you mean, before I *offed* Seixas. . . ."

"I didn't hear you say that," went Gonsalves. "You were understandably jealous. A matter of temporary insanity. Whatever . . ."

"That's what the Jamaicans are saying," I pointed out. "You'll have to do better."

Gonsalves said, "We'll arrange for interviews. Dick Cavett or Bill Moyers on Public Broadcasting, and the like. A case can be made Seixas was a double, and you found out, and were only doing your patriotic best. Your thing. Give us some time to think. We'll fix it. I know we can. We always do."

"And what about the Jamaicans?" I asked. "What will they be doing?"

"They talk a lot of left-wing talk," Gonsalves said, "but they really need us Americans. They need our brains, and our technology.

"Besides," he added, "you're not like them. You're one of us. A western mind. . . . They still live in the stone age down here, like gorillas."

I frowned.

He was asking me to be this happy, well-adjusted racist, like him, serving all the Imperial domains.

I was pretty amazed because when I had considered myself a good servant of all that nobody had ever noticed me.

Gonsalves seemed to feel he had presented his case with eminent clarity, and generosity.

He was now inspecting a tiny food spot on the cuff of his otherwise immaculate trousers. It was a sort of reddish brown. Could have been blood—or shit.

He scratched away at the thing with his fingernail, without much success.

At last when he looked up again with a slightly defeated air, I said, "You mean to say I am to go back just as before, with no strings?"

"The Agency needs to have people placed like you in important situations, but I think you will find," Gonsalves added, "we are nowhere near as possessive as some. . . ."

"How do you know I won't try and double on you?"

"You can if you like, and we'd know," he said, "but you won't, because you're an American patriot, sir, aren't you?"

"And the money?"

"You made a good enough living teaching. You never really wanted any more than that, and you won't need any more. If you have any expenses of course they'll be reimbursed."

"And the fame?"

"That wasn't your *shtick* either, Professor. We know a lot about you. In our terms you're a decent, honest tough-minded man."

"Can I write all about what happened?"

"Just as you like," he told me, "just so long as it's a 'novel.' We certainly wouldn't ever want to interfere with your academic freedoms, but we do have certain rules. You understand. . . ."

I thought I did.

He knew I did. He had me.

I was beginning to know just about the same things.

I said, "Any friend of yours is a friend of mine."

"Precisely the way I've been feeling," Gonsalves said, up toward the ceiling.

There was only one more piece of business to get settled. I asked if Gonsalves could do anything for my colleague, Blake.

"What? The fellow who wants to blow *everybody's* cover?"

"The very one," I said. "I'd like him to get another chance, too."

Gonsalves gnawed at his lower lip, as if deep in thought.

"You're a loyal person and we like that about you," he said, "but frankly, Blake is a horse's ass and deserves everything he's getting.

"With what he knew," he said, "if he'd been a little nicer about things, it would have been different. All he had to do was invite his Chairman to dinner at Butler Hall and tell him what he knew and they'd have made him full Professor, just like that. But he chose to go public, a very stupid thing to do, from a realistic point of view."

"Is there no way?" I asked. "After all, I'll have to face Blake, among others, when I get back."

"Tell you what," he said. "We'll offer him a Fulbright teaching year in Rome. Do you think that will buy him off?"

"No."

"Then he can go stuff it," Gonsalves said. "And you too, I'm afraid."

I had overplayed my hand.

"Wait a minute," I told him. "I was only asking. No harm in asking, is there?"

Gonsalves let his face relax and smiled at me benevolently, again.

"The real reason why we like you, Professor," he said, "is you're not so loyal to anybody that you don't know what reality is all about. Now as to your friend with literary problems . . ."

So Blake went to the Aspen Institute for one summer and then became Fulbright Professor of American History in Managua, Nicaragua for a year, after which he was promoted by Columbia, and by the time his little monograph appeared, certain names were deleted, with the consent of Agency, and author.

And that's pretty much the way it all ended, happily enough, for Blake, and me, and Dyllis, and our gang of friends.

In my diaries I have noted: "History repeats itself: the first time as tragedy, and the second time as the taste of delicatessen in McLean, Virginia."

Twenty minutes later that same day Gonsalves and I went out that same hotel room door together with my suitcases and nobody even tried to stop us.

At the American Embassy we were driven by limousine to the airport and escorted through customs, without any questions.

From Kingston I was flown by unmarked Lear Jet to Vieques, P.R., debriefed, polygraphed, fluttered, and flattered. After much swearing of inchoate oaths, I was decorated with various Agency medallions, but was only allowed to keep a small red, white, and blue ribbon of gold which I wear in the eye-hole lapel of my best grey suit, even to this day.

A week later I flew back to New York and went home again.

There was a brief flurry of interest from the press, but when it was explained that I could not possibly answer any questions about a case still pending before the Jamaican courts, the interest in me died down perfunctorily.

In the fall I began to teach at Columbia again.

Jamaica dropped its charges against me a year or so later, and I was given my own endowed chair, made possible through a grant from a benefactor who preferred to remain anonymous.

I've seen Dyllis once or twice since then, but we have very little to say to each other except wham bam thank you ma'am, which doesn't seem very appropriate in our case, though we still do it.

In our circle asking a lot of questions is considered quite bad form.

I do my work, have a house near the Hamptons at Louse Point, where I worked on this "novel," among other things.

Every month or so I get postcards from Pullman. He's back in Cuba now, managing one of their baseball teams.

He says the life is pretty dull, but he's happy with Marina, even though he never signs any of his cards.

How do I know it's him?

Who else would a man like me know in Cuba?

The last time he wrote, Randall Pullman said he still considered me a Revolutionist, in case I cared to know; in specifics he charged me with being a "left social democrat of anarchistic tendencies."

Most of the time my Havana correspondent just writes in crypto, i.e., "CO5 encaustic patterns" was a characteristic recent message.

Also, "To a valuable asset, Best regards."

Well, I don't pretend to know what that's all about, though, if you were to ask me, even now, I would probably say, business as usual, singly, or doubly. But any friend of his is most definitely *not* a friend of mine, under any circumstances.

Frankly, I don't even know what the hell the whole scam was all about. Can't even pretend to know. A couple of weeks lost in my life amounted to an education in reality, the practical side of life: I learned what it was like to get a bullet in the ass, some nice warm sex, and live with a lot of fear.

Now I'm considered a first-class teacher. My students say I'm funny and knowledgeable. They also say I seem to be more worldly than most of the others they run up against, but they probably say the same things about them, too, when I'm not around.

Hell, we all work for the same employers, don't we?

Whenever I find somebody who is really promising, whether he or she, I invite the person to my place for a drink, or coffee in a cup, and we talk.

Perhaps I can do them a good turn.

No strings attached.

I throw a lot of parties for the people in my crowd, and

there's always a few interesting young strangers who get invited and make a hit.

I only wish sometimes I were more ambitious. They would probably make me editor of one of our leading quarterlies.

The trouble is sometimes at night. I hear a hectic reggae beat. The words of that tune crowd out all my other thoughts:

> *"Mr. Seixas go bang bang*
> *Professor Harmon go bang bang*
> *The Agency it do believe*
> *Dangerous to be naive. . . ."*